DARK HORSES

The Magazine of Weird Fiction

JANUARY | 2023

No. 12

CONTENTS

NIGHT VISION

Brad Petit

Henkin is recruited because he has experience in stealing things. So he says. Obviously Frost is worried about the extra risk— supposing Henkin gets caught, suppose he flips—but there's more risk in going it alone. A worse risk, meaning. The risk of failure. Frost doesn't know what he's doing and that more or less settles that.

They meet through a mutual friend. When Frost asks the friend for a reference, being vague on the details, the friend thinks about it for a minute and then writes down a phone number on the back of some receipt from his pocket.

"Trustworthy?" Frost asks.

"Seeing as I don't know what you're up to I can't answer that," the friend says.

Then Henkin and Frost have their first meeting in the plaza downtown as arranged, Henkin making Frost wait too long. It starts to feel like a prank or a setup. But Henkin glides over across the brick surface, tall and lean, and stops at Frost's bench for a bit before saying, "Should we go somewhere?"

It's a game of chicken to see who'll bring up the job first, which Frost finally does over sandwiches. Henkin has already let Frost pay for their food when he hands him a five dollar bill right before they part ways. Only later does Frost see it's a fake, and he suspects that Henkin knows that he knows. So that's all right.

"This is the back door," Frost says. He turns off the headlights but there's still some visibility just from whatever stray light is around.

"I can see that," Henkin says.

Frost keeps his hands on the steering wheel. They're parked uncomfortably close to the building. He has trouble even looking at it. He's still shaken from the traffic stop they pass on the way over, the way the officer glances at him as they roll by and there's something in his grin that reminds Frost they've met before, but only Frost knows it.

"They all go home by six o'clock unless there's an evening service," he says.

"And how will we know if there is one?"

"We won't."

"We could read the obituaries."

Frost stares forward, realizing of course that not everyone buys an obit but not bothering to point it out. He's the one in charge and he doesn't need to argue.

"I think the middle of the night would be best anyway," he says.

"Janitor?"

"I don't know."

"Of course you don't."

The telephone rings at seven-thirty in the morning. No one calls at this hour—no one calls much at all. Frost looks at his watch on the nightstand before picking up the phone. It probably rings eight or more times.

Henkin starts in right away. "There you are," he says.

Frost murmurs something back.

"Listen," Henkin says. "It's about your vehicle. You realize it's much too small."

"Well what about yours?" Frost says.

"You hired me and strictly me," Henkin says. He sounds like a hardass bureaucrat, someone who gets off on technicalities.

Frost yawns into the phone and twists himself upright, seated on the edge of the bed, with his bare feet hovering in between the floor and the ends of his pajama pants, a gift from his mother. On Henkin's end of the line there's the sound of a news report and the hard scraping of a spoon against a bowl. But no chewing.

"I'll work on it," Frost says.

"Yeah, work on it." The news announces unrest in South America.

Frost scratches at his side.

"So how long've you had these visions?" Henkin says.

Frost is caught off guard. He's mute for a minute and then says, "What? Who said anything about that?"

"Relax," Henkin says, drawing it out. "I'm not going to tell anyone. It's not like I care. I just don't see how pinching one of these boxes is going to do anything about it."

"I don't—"

"Fine, have it your way." Henkin knocks on the bowl some more. "Do you have dimensions? Casket ain't small, you realize. We need a truck, better yet a van. If you need a hot one just tell me."

"No—stop. Don't say that on the phone. Christ, you shouldn't even be calling me."

Henkin makes a soft clicking noise with his mouth. He's imitating a tap. Then he laughs. "Don't flatter yourself," he says. "No one cares what you're saying."

Frost is about to reply to that when Henkin hangs up. For an instant the rattle makes Frost think the receiver has gotten loose and is falling apart against his ear. In his room the smell of old laundry taints the air, but Frost hardly notices this anymore and he lays back down trying unsuccessfully to sleep again.

Never before has Frost seen a man so large or so sallow. He steps out of the van like it's birthing him. It's the man's idea to meet in the parking lot in front of the grocery and hardware stores and the florist, which to Frost feels too public, too exposed, but the man insists. On the phone he says to call him Rupp. He grabs a stray shopping cart near where he's parked and as he walks it over toward Frost it looks like some novelty item, tiny at the end of his huge hands like that.

"See?" Rupp says. "Kind of more subtle than the underpass."

Frost tries not to look around too obviously, to check if anyone is watching them. No one can help staring at a giant man like this. It's the middle of the day and the wives, children, and old people are out. The temperature is mild but Frost feels like he might start to sweat.

"Is that the van?" he asks. He nods toward it.

Rupp takes another half stride forward. Frost feels himself almost step back. A police vehicle and a hearse pass each other on the roadway behind him, travelling in opposite directions.

"A beauty isn't she," Rupp says. "Plenty of life in her yet."

"How much?"

"Well. Henkin *did* say you were in a spot."

Frost stiffens. "That's not exactly true."

Rupp's mouth turns into a big meaty smirk. Frost sees him eating straight from tin cans, balanced on a folding chair in his kitchen, his weight slowly crushing it with every new spoonful. He sees himself inspecting the back of the van at the man's invitation and coming out in bags. It's the first time he imagines it happening that way, but it feels as real as a memory. He looks at the van and his sudden thought is to buy it so he can destroy it.

"So how much?" Frost says.

"How much do you have? Right now."

He sees the oversized hand separate from the shopping cart handle and move backward, slowly like it's trying to move through water, and reach behind for Rupp's waistband. A release of fear dumps itself into Frost's body not unlike his early orgasms and he stumbles away, falling toward his own car. By the time he sees that Rupp only means to scratch his back Frost is already committed to the escape. He might mutter some kind of excuse along the way, but more likely he doesn't.

"All right," Henkin says over the phone. "We can use mine. And it's going to cost you extra."

"Fine," Frost says.

"Unless you want me to steal us a meat wagon. Which I can do but it will cost extra again."

"No," Frost says quickly. That's not the plan—that's going too far.

Henkin is quiet for a moment, looking in cabinets.

"Relax. I didn't mean it. What a great way for us to get pinched, driving around in that thing. You think I'm that dumb?"

Maybe. How is Frost supposed to know?

They settle on Monday for the attempt. Tuesday morning, technically. Henkin runs down a list of supplies he expects Frost to have, then says he'll provide half of them anyway. He hangs up without asking if they're done.

Frost looks at the phone then unplugs it. After taking off his wristwatch he crosses the bedroom and opens the window. That doesn't quite do it—he opens two more windows in the front room. Then he opens the front door and stands on his stoop and finally the pressure goes from his temples. The neighbor kids are still playing outside even though it's getting past dusk.

He dreams it another way that night: the long black car filling up with water, the coffin in the back bobbing around and knocking against the tint windows, Henkin smiling at him and blowing his own brains out before the waterline can reach his jaw.

The crowbar gets them in the building easily enough. Henkin seems good at using them. The air inside has the smell of potpourri unsettled by something metallic. Frost can hear himself breathing, and he only breathes louder the more he tries not to. When Henkin flicks on his long, heavy flashlight they see they're in a big storage room lined with racks for buckets, boxes, empty picture frames. Henkin pushes the door closed behind them, feeling carefully for where the latch catches.

"The showroom is down the hall to the left," he says.

"Wait," Frost says. "What if someone's here?"

Henkin gestures at a rack loaded with candlesticks.

"You crack him on the head with one of those."

"What if they're armed?"

"Then someone beat us to the job. Don't be ridiculous."

Frost lets Henkin go ahead of him. They come out of the storage room at the end of a wide hallway with furniture spread along the walls, plush seats and small sofas for the bereaved to rest upon. Henkin sweeps his flashlight up and down like an experienced cat burglar. He spits on the carpet and starts for the other end of the hall.

The showroom is smaller than Frost thinks it will be. The caskets are arranged in a horseshoe before them, six in total. They're on stands or catafalques of some kind and the stands are surrounded by little curtains. The metal handles and trim on the caskets sparkle dully from the flashlight, the wood deep and stained. Frost feels his pulse in his chest and his lungs seem half their size. It's dark but he can sense the caskets pressing toward him but he does not retreat. Henkin stands ahead of him, surveying the room.

"Take your pick," he says. "The lighter the better. I'll go find the trolley."

Frost is alone in the showroom for less than a minute when Henkin comes rushing back to the doorway.

"What the hell have you done?" he says, his voice urgent and angry. He stares hard at Frost from above the hard angles of his cheekbones.

"What?"

"There're here and you're the only person who could have told them."

Frost is confused. Henkin isn't making any sense.

"Who?" Frost says. His pulse is still banging in his rib cage, his throat.

Henkin reaches out and grabs him by the shirt. He's holding the flashlight in his other hand, aiming its beam at the ground. "Take a look for yourself, sweetheart." He yanks Frost out of the showroom and back into the hallway.

The hallway runs along the front edge of the building, the street edge. It's bathed in blue and red in the darkness, flashing with color from the lights blazing outside the windows of the place.

"Cops!" Frost says.

"Just like you planned it," Henkin says. "How much did they offer you? Well it's not going to matter now."

Frost begins to stumble backward but Henkin pulls on his shirt again. He hasn't let go.

"Now wait a minute," Frost says. He grabs Henkin's wrist. "Hey. Hey!" There's a panic in Frost's face as he struggles against Henkin's grasp on him, and then his eyes go wide. "It was you!"

Henkin glances up and down the hallway. The way they've come in is down at the same end near where the cops are parked. Probably, the cops have the place surrounded by now.

"Tell you what," Henkin says. He drives Frost back through the door of the showroom. "We'll fight over who gets to play detective later. Right now, you make yourself disappear behind one of these things while I go see what we're up against."

Standing just inside the doorway to the showroom Henkin is little more than a dark figure framed by the dim smears of violet jumping around in the hallway beyond. Frost wants to object but he doesn't know what else to do. He swallows, nods, and turns around to go hide.

After Henkin delivers the first blow to Frost's head with the flashlight he steps back to let Frost's body slump to the floor. Then he kneels down next to him and clubs him a few more times, raising the flashlight up high and bringing it down as hard as possible. He stands and watches the body twitch on the floor and then it looks to be a done deal. It's quiet in the showroom, no sound of breathing at all. The caskets float above their curtains in an indifferent way, and as he looks at them Henkin feels a wave of contempt rise up then recede, like a wave at a beach. He wipes the flashlight with one of the curtains, rebalances it in his hand, and switches it off.

He keeps the van below the speed limit driving home, using his blinkers, keeping a mind out for things he can't see. He's got his hands at ten and two when the lights from the car behind him reflect across the bridge of his nose, and as his eyes shift to the mirror the car pulls quietly into the other lane and then it's gone.

PINK ON PINK

Mary Jo Rabe

Marianne DuBois ran her fingers through her short, dark hair. She was used to keeping everything under complete control, but the pervasive, caustic, Martian dust wreaked havoc on her carefully and perfectly coiffed hair.

There was much she already loved about her new life on Mars, but it took all of her willpower to look in the mirror before leaving her apartment.

She sighed and told herself to concentrate on the positive. Her apartment, close to the bottom of the one of the cliffs of the Valles Marineris, was small but efficiently furnished and generously supplied with state-of-the-art appliances. More importantly, it was well ventilated to keep out the stench of Martian dust. She considered it perfect for the time being.

The first thing she did when she moved in was to clear a space on the floor for her meditation circle, about one and a half meters in diameter. She then had a decorator robot come and paint it a bright, shocking pink, her favorite color and, as it happened, her power color. Then she got an electrician robot to install a pink spotlight above the circle.

Most apartments were completely underground, but Marianne had a reinforced plastic, outside window. She needed to observe the planet from its surface as well as to absorb impressions from underground. The Valles Marineris changed its contours with every dust storm, and she loved watching the games the transient flows of dust played on the rocks.

The entire northern cliff of the Valles Marineris was filled with tunnels. All Marianne had to do was go out her apartment door some twenty stories beneath the Martian surface and she could travel to any location on the planet that had been modified and made safe for human habitation.

Swift robot vehicles meant that she didn't even need to fly.

Marianne had quickly adjusted to many of the changes in her new life in the Bradbury habitat, lower gravity that made her clumsy and uncoordinated instead of lissome and graceful, near-vacuum surface conditions fatal for human life forms, time-delayed technological communication with planet Earth that made it slow and expensive to chat with friends and professional associates.

But she would never get used to what planet Mars did to her appearance. Her stiff hair stuck out in all directions, the Martian dust dried her skin to leather no matter how much she oiled it, and her figure bulged in an unsightly manner, bloated from random and inconveniently located collections of fluid.

It wasn't vanity. As a fashion designer, a profession and calling that she loved, her appearance was her meal ticket. In order to sell people the apparel she designed, she had to create an illusion of beauty.

The easiest way was to act as her own fashion model, at least that's how she had done it on Earth, for more years than her customers ever suspected. She had long been successful at keeping this body in optimal working condition including the respective appearance of a young woman.

Naturally she had certain other methods at her disposal for creating illusions; she could indeed make people see an adolescent fashion model when they looked at her, but TANSTAAFL. Even witches had to balance the magic they used against the energy they lost.

Finding access to the secret Martian forces of nature as well as determining the amount of such magical energy available on Mars was what she was sent here to do. Witches, being immortal for all practical purposes when supplied with sources of natural magic, tended to think long-term. That's why the coven had paid her way. The decision, however, had been somewhat controversial, and so she was under pressure to succeed.

Marianne glanced at the short, stocky, middle-aged woman in the full-length mirror on the door to the bath cubicle. Her standard-issue, one-piece, grayish coveralls were not flattering. She doubted that this garb would look good on anyone. The only thing worse than the standard-issue habitat clothes were the surface spacesuits. They made everyone look fat and ungainly.

Ugly clothing was bad for habitat morale. Always had been, always would be. People who felt unattractive didn't work effectively or enthusiastically. At least that's what she had been able to convince the billionaire of when she applied to be a colonist in the settlement the old man was bankrolling. She promised him that fashionably attired colonists would make his settlement solvent before he knew it.

Time to get to work. Now that she was on Mars, she had to show what she could do, which happened to be what she loved to do. For her it was just a formality that all new colonists had to demonstrate the value of their contributions to the settlement if they wanted to stay beyond their probationary period.

Marianne wanted to succeed and loved her fashion work. In addition, it was obvious to her that the colonists here desperately needed her talents. Surely no one could stand wearing these ugly clothes much longer.

There were, however, also the demands from her coven. Still, she could only concentrate on one thing at a time.

She pulled out her standard-issue communicator and fumbled around until she managed to order a robot vehicle to take her to the Stevensen Plastics factory where she had her first appointment today. Before she could start designing clothes, she had to find out precisely which materials the factory was willing to create for her and how much they would cost.

The gray, plastic robot vehicle reminded her of a fragile dune buggy, four narrow seats, a frame instead of a roof. Too bad it probably wasn't sturdy enough for maneuvering over the dunes on the Martian surface. She guessed that the dashboard was the robot driver or at least the software interface, and so she climbed in and pressed what she hoped was the right button on her communication device.

The vehicle accelerated quickly to an impressive speed and tore off through the tunnels. It would have been a pleasant ride except for the annoying whining noise from the electric motor. After a few minutes Marianne closed her eyes and started chanting to herself and to whatever powers might be listening in order to block out the electromagnetic moaning. She had long since lost any sense of direction and was starting to feel slightly claustrophobic in the tunnels.

When the vehicle stopped at the first entrance to the plastics factory, a door opened, and a tall, slender, assured woman with long, white hair, also dressed in ill-fitting, gray coveralls, walked over to the vehicle and said, "Ms. DuBois, I'm Miranda Stevensen. It's good to finally meet you in person after all our correspondence. Come in, and we can talk about how we can help you."

Marianne awkwardly climbed out of the vehicle and stumbled behind Ms. Stevensen, whose office was small, yet cozy rather than claustrophobic. The scenes from the Martian surface on the fake, holographic windows helped. Ms. Stevensen sat behind her narrow desk and motioned for Marianne to sit on the other side. The dark-red, plastic chair that welcomed her was surprisingly comfortable, especially the cushiony fabric cover that felt like wool but had to be plastic.

Marianne stroked the luxurious armrests. "This feels amazing," she said. "And all of this is plastic?"

Ms. Stevensen smiled. "We had to learn how to produce things, including fabric, from the natural resources available here on Mars," she said. "There may never be any animals on Mars, and the settlement's economy only allows for growing plants that people can eat, but there are plenty of chemicals we can work with. It continues to be a fascinating learning process."

"Then you can produce whatever fabrics I need?" Marianne asked.

"That we can," Ms. Stevensen said. "However, you might want to do the necessary research to determine just what your fabrics have to be good for. What kind of clothes were you planning on selling here?"

"All kinds," Marianne said. "I want to make working clothes, leisure clothes, fun clothes. I'll also have to produce footwear, shoes and boots. No offence, but the ugly clodhoppers everyone is wearing here won't be suitable as accessories for my clothing lines."

"None taken," Ms. Stevensen said. "No one thinks these standard-issue clothes or shoes are attractive. However, they are practical, and you should keep that aspect in mind for your designs."

"Good point," Marianne agreed. "I think I've got that covered, practical, comfortable, but also pleasing to the eye. Once I get the habitat clothing business going well enough, I also want to try my hand at making surface suits. But I'll definitely talk to the physicists and planetologists about that first."

"I don't want to discourage you at all," Ms. Stevensen said. "And it will make us happy to sell you as much fabric as you can use, but I think you also need to talk to the chemists about the habitat clothes. One of the settlement regulations specifies that each member of the habitat has to be able to slip into a surface suit within five minutes of an alarm going off. The habitat clothing can't get in the way."

"You must have noticed the dust by now," she continued. "It's everywhere and will affect how the fabrics feel on your skin and how they look and feel after they've been laundered."

"You're right, and I will," Marianne said. "But let's still talk numbers. How I would like to proceed is that I'll describe what I want the fabrics to look and feel like, you'll make me samples, and then I'll place my initial order or ask for changes."

"Sounds good," Ms. Stevensen said. "How are you planning to get all these clothes made, sold, and delivered?"

"Robots," Marianne answered. "My next stop is to talk to Layla Jahoob. I was told she could design and produce robots that could do anything. I need robot seamstresses."

"I will only sell custom-made clothing. My customers will tell me what they think they want, the robots will get precise measurements, and I will design the perfect attire. Then the customers can pick up the finished products or I can have a robot deliver them."

"And what about returns?" Ms. Stevensen asked. "When people want to dispose of their used garments, you should have the cloth returned to us. We do have to recycle almost everything here on Mars."

"Certainly," Marianne agreed. "And I assume you will recycle these fabrics in such a way that you make a profit on selling the new fabrics you then produce from them. It would only be fair for you to then reduce the price of the next fabric orders I place."

"Fair and obviously good business practice," Ms. Stevensen said as she smiled again. "Then I can only wish you all the best. Give us your fabric, and we'll produce the samples. Naturally we'll need a down payment in settlement credits before we can begin, but I assume that's not a problem."

Marianne knew a down payment wasn't a problem. The only problem could be if the scaredy-cats in her coven back on

Earth started joining their familiars in self-induced panic attacks. Witches were notoriously inconsistent and unreliable. She would have to remind them: The decision was made, and now they were "in for a potion, in for a cauldron."

The potential benefits to all Wiccans from her successful stay on Mars couldn't be measured in any human currency, and so her coven would simply have to pay the billionaire what he demanded so that he would add that amount to her settlement credits. She knew full well that her coven alone had more than enough cash stashed away. More importantly, Marianne was impatient to get her business started.

"No problem," Marianne said. "I'll send you my descriptions and you can reply stating the amount of credits you need."

Marianne punched at her communicator. "Could you help me call for another robot car?" she asked. "I still don't have the hang of these devices."

Ms. Stevensen was helpful, and Marianne was soon on her way to the robot manufacturers.

Layla Jahoob didn't have an office; she had multiple tables at one end of a gigantic warehouse. Like every other room in the settlement, the walls were gray, but the printers and other loud machines in front of them displayed every color of the visual spectrum that human beings could recognize.

The noise was somewhat deafening, clanks and screeches at irregular intervals. The floor was overrun with robots being herded by what she suspected were human employees since they wore headsets. Ms. Jahoob, short and stocky like Marianne but with significantly better developed muscles, also wore a black headset, though it got lost in her thick, curly hair. She handed one to Marianne as soon as she entered the warehouse.

"Doc Brach says it's too loud in here and we need to wear noise protection," Ms. Jahoob explained, her voice loud and clear in Marianne's headset. "Apparently his medical nanobots can repair damaged hearing, but undamaged is better. How can I help you?"

Marianne glanced at the tables, three meters long and one meter wide, which seemed to be 3-D computer touch screens. Geometric figures danced in and out of existence, followed by sequences of numbers. The view was vaguely hypnotic, and Marianne had to force herself to look away.

"I need seamstress robots," she began. Ms. Jahoob stared at her quizzically, and Marianne explained her idea about producing custom-made, attractive but comfortable clothing for everyone who lived and worked on Mars.

Ms. Jahoob moved to a table against the wall and slid her stubby fingers over a virtual keyboard. She looked back at Marianne. "Come and look at my numbers," she said. "I'd like to make a rough estimate considering the number of current and projected colonists and how long the fabrics you use will last, that is to say, how often robots will be busy making new items of clothing. What else do I need to factor in?"

"Shelf-life of fashion," Marianne said automatically. "Once all the settlers have their first sets of clothes, I'll be introducing new styles about once a Martian year. And, of course, people's sizes may change over time."

"Hmm," Ms. Jahoob mumbled. "I think you'll need your own little sewing factory with space for ten robots to work and a small area for your customers to try on the finished clothes."

"How many sewing machines?" Marianne asked.

"None," Ms. Jahoob answered. "The robots themselves will have appendages that do all fabric assembly work. You'll just have to give me precise documentation of every action a robot needs to take to cut and fasten the materials correctly. The standard AI programming will allow for additional sewing instructions and the robots themselves will learn from every garment they create and reprogram themselves accordingly."

"Okay," Marianne said. "You're the expert. When can you give me my robots?"

"First I think you will need builder robots to construct your little sewing room addition to the habitat. It would be cheapest to put it on the surface. We would just have to put a safety door in an outside wall and build a little dome for your production and sales area. Once we have this, the robots can get started."

"Sounds good," Marianne said. "Can you take care of all the formalities involved?"

"No problem," Ms. Jahoob answered. "The mayor of the settlement is a stupid, obnoxious jerk, but we know how to work around him. That's how anyone gets anything done around here."

Marianne really didn't want to bother with questions of architecture and habitat building regulations. She had the feeling that Ms. Jahoob was competent to get this done for her. "When can you get started?"

"I'll send you an estimate of costs and the down payment we require," Ms. Jahoob said. "We will start as soon as we get your credits transfer."

Having gotten half the things done that she wanted to do, Marianne managed to summon a robot car to take her back to her apartment. Once there she grabbed a bottle of reprocessed Martian water out of her little refrigerator. It tasted slightly bleachy, but she was thirsty and managed to swallow all of it.

Then it was on to her other task. She switched on the pink spotlight, walked over to her pink circle, and knelt in the center. As always, the power of the pink refreshed and fortified her. She had been on Mars for a while now, and she sensed that it was time to attempt her other task here.

She emptied her mind, at least as much as possible, and tried to connect telepathically with the natural powers of the red planet. She waited patiently, but sensed nothing. She felt coldness and slowness from inside the planet. The sensations surrounded her in her circle, but there was nothing more.

This was going to be more challenging than she thought. However, it did make sense. Mars was a cold planet; the volcanic fires had long since cooled to a freezing point. There was chemically contaminated water, but only in sluggish, frosty, little underground pools, each one too far from the other for good communication.

The only steady natural power was the wispy wind, but maybe she was thinking too parochially. She had to reach out to powers here on Mars that no one had thought to connect with on Earth, like the cosmic radiation beating down onto the surface.

However, at the moment she was too exhausted to make a new attempt. To be honest, finding magic on Mars was never her top priority, and so she was more than willing to wait.

She called up a robot car and booked passage to the cafeteria. She needed some decent food, and it would be a good idea to start making contact with future customers. Emma, the cafeteria lady, has been very kind when Marianne was there before. The panorama view of the surface of Mars from the above-ground cafeteria would also give her ideas for the new clothes she wanted to design.

Hanging out in the cafeteria turned out to be a good idea. Emma insisted on introducing her to everyone who came in. People were thrilled by the idea that they could finally have better-looking clothes that were comfortable and fit perfectly. One of the teenagers quickly set up a little spreadsheet for Marianne to enter all the orders into.

Marianne was surprised, but Emma explained it to her. Settlers were paid a fairly generous salary and there just wasn't that much to spend your money on. Accommodations, food, and medical care were part of the salary package. Theoretically, you could spend more on better accommodations, but the luxury living areas hadn't been constructed yet.

Eventually, people got tired of only spending money on guided tours of the planet. So, they liked the idea of being able to buy luxury items like nice clothes.

The people she talked to said they wanted all kinds of clothes and in every imaginable color, including Marianne's favorite hot pink. They weren't as certain about what kind of cloth they wanted, though. Marianne made a note for Ms. Jahoob. The robot sewing room would need an extra space for customers to walk around and touch the different fabrics.

When she got back to her apartment, Marianne sent off orders for Ms. Stevensen and Ms. Jahoob. She decided to order more square meters of fabric than she had originally thought because she came up with all kinds of new textures. She told Ms. Jahoob that she would need a larger room than originally planned for the robots, fabrics, and for her customers. Now that she was going to do this, she was going to do it right.

Late the next day fabric samples arrived which were excellent. The day after that, estimates and requests for down payments showed up in her communicator. They were significantly higher than she had expected. The settlement credits she already had in her business account wouldn't even be enough for one down payment.

She couldn't put it off any longer. It was time to call the coven.

Video chat to Earth was quite pricey, but now unavoidable. Fortunately the planets were so aligned that the time gap was only about six minutes. First she sent a text asking all twelve to assemble at a predetermined time. She waited and then tapped the code for Mars-Earth communication into the wall communicator, another one of the perks of her apartment, a two-by-one-meter wall video screen.

As soon as she saw the twelve faces of her coven members, she read them the estimates for the costs of setting up her clothing business and announced how much Earth currency the coven would have to transfer to the old billionaire asap.

None of the twelve faces looked happy, probably because she had taken so long to get in touch with them. Five looked definitely hostile, even though it would take at least six minutes before they heard what she said. Marianne couldn't expect any benevolent consideration or reflection from this crowd.

To be fair, Marianne had never had the best witchly reputation. The others suspected, justifiably, that her heart wasn't really in the witch business. She enjoyed her mortal exploits too much. However, in the final analysis, that was why they were willing to send her to Mars. She was considered the least talented of the coven, the one they could most easily do without if they had to.

Marianne herself had just wanted the adventure of traveling to Mars. Being able to run her clothing design business without any interference from the coven, however, was a welcome extra.

Marianne tried to meditate while she waited for the delayed answer. This was not going to be a happy conversation.

Some fifteen minutes later, the video screen activated again.

Ulrika, the most hostile figure on the screen whose mouth looked like she had been sucking on a lemon, spoke first. "That is completely unacceptable. You need to bargain for a better price."

Marianne sighed. The old witch was just as unreasonable as she expected.

"No can do," Marianne answered. "The settlement on Mars has a monopoly economy. No business here has any competition; it's all 'take it or leave it'. If you want to bargain with the old billionaire, feel free, as long as I get this amount in settlement credits to start my business with."

"So, I think it is a waste of everybody's time to argue about this. We voted to have me go to Mars and start a legitimate, mortal business here. Once I succeeded at that, I was to investigate the possibilities for tapping into the Martian natural forces to see if they would provide sufficient magic for our coven or even for all interested Wiccans."

Then Marianne sat back and waited for her message to get through to them. About fifteen minutes later the video screen moved.

"Yes," Marie, one of the more flexible Wiccans, said. Today she had the appearance of a young, blonde cheerleader. Marianne wondered vaguely if that was the result of conscious effort or magic. "We understand that your business is necessary and that you need start-up funds. However, don't forget that your top priority is still to investigate the possible presence of magical powers on Mars. There may very well come a time when we perhaps will not be able to continue living on Earth."

Marianne thought for a moment. Her immediate task was to get the coven to transfer the funds, not to argue about priorities.

"Then let's not waste any more time," she said. "Get the money to old Ned Baxter, and tell him to get it credited to my account here so I can get my business going. That will take time, just like connecting with the powers of nature here will, assuming there are any."

While she was waiting, Marianne began sketching and doodling. As an afterthought, she called up habitat regulations on her hand-held communicator to see to what extent attire was regulated. There were a few safety and medical aspects she hadn't given enough thought to, especially with regard to footwear and surface suits.

Ulrika finally came back on the screen. "Just what progress have you made in connecting with the natural powers of the planet?" she asked. "After all, that's the reason we're paying for your little jaunt."

Marianne sighed. This was getting tiresome.

"I've gotten started; I've sent feelers out into the planet," Marianne said. This was true, although she had so far only made one attempt. However, the coven didn't need to know everything. "So far there is nothing to report. In the interests of cost-cutting wherever possible, I'll end this conversation now and notify you when the necessary funds are credited to my settlement account, and I can have my first clothes produced."

Marianne hoped that would be sufficient to keep Ulrika from continuing her arguments. Ulrika had been skeptical about choosing Marianne to go to Mars. And she had always had nothing but contempt for Marianne's clothing design business on Earth. No wonder. Ulrika always insisted on dressing like a dull and drab Halloween witch. Marianne wouldn't put it past her to try to sabotage the whole Mars project.

Three Martian days later, Marianne got the news that sufficient credits had been deposited in her business account.

She immediately transferred the requested credits for her fabrics, robots, and the addition to the surface habitat building.

Feeling happy and optimistic, she turned on the pink spotlight and knelt down in the middle of her pink circle. As always, the pink soothed and strengthened her. She emptied her mind and tried to feel her way into the depths of the planet. This time she sensed something from the planet, some excruciatingly slow response almost too faint for her to be sure it was there. Obviously, this was going to take a lot more time. In the meantime, she had to get her business going.

The production area/showroom addition to the habitat was completed in record time. The fabric production took longer since Marianne had ordered a large variety of fabric types, colors, and designs.

This wasn't a bad thing; it gave Marianne plenty of time to test the robots' skills on patterns she printed off on the gray pseudo-paper people used on Mars. The robotic seamstress software didn't work perfectly at the beginning, but after several days the robots were indeed capable of transforming her patterns into paper clothes that would fit human beings.

Ulrika insisted on regular coven meetings, noting that Marianne surely now had more than enough settlement credits to pay for the video calls. Marianne reported dutifully about the slow but steady progress she was making with the Martian powers of nature without mentioning that it was more slow than steady. She deliberately said less and less about her clothing business. The other witches weren't interested in it anyway.

Marianne was happy with the fabrics once they were delivered; they looked and felt like top quality plant and animal material from Earth. Her customers were even more enthusiastic, and they were absolutely thrilled when they saw the finished clothes. Marianne's clothing business was turning out to be successful beyond her wildest dreams.

Despite all the other demands on her time, Marianne spent at least an hour a day observing the surface, watching the dust storms and dust devils. Every couple of days, she rode one of the tour buses to see the landscape farther away from the habitat, the dunes, the crevices, the ancient volcanoes. Every view of Mars gave her new ideas for her clothes.

More and more, she also enjoyed the time she spent meditating in her pink circle, gaining strength from the pink. There were indeed natural powers in the cold depths of the planet and in the toasty radiation from the rest of the universe striking the surface. She couldn't communicate with them directly yet, but she had the impression that they were evaluating her, maybe even getting used to her.

She felt she needed a more direct contact with the planet, so she consulted with the scientists in the habitat to get ideas for less oppressive surface suits. With new plastics from the Stevensen factories she was able to construct tight, plastic suits with hoods that connected to oxygen sources. The plastic threads that crisscrossed the suits in a fine mesh reflected some forms of radiation and absorbed others to provide heat to the suits.

She tested all the versions of the suit herself, relying exclusively on her mortal powers. After hours of intrusive medical tests, Doc Brach then certified the suits as safe for at least eight uninterrupted hours on the surface. With every hour she spent walking on the surface, she felt her time in her pink circle bring her closer to the original powers of the planet Mars. More and more, she sensed an overpowering strength emanating from the core of the planet.

However, since she still didn't have any direct communication with the powers of nature, in her conversations with the coven she downplayed her progress. Ulrika was getting unbearable. Marianne was tired of her sarcasm and her threats, the newest of which was that Ulrika would come to Mars herself and take over from Marianne, since Marianne was obviously bungling the whole mission.

Her clothing business did better and better. One of her youthful fans insisted on broadcasting shows of her productions, and the demand for her clothes from Earth developed. At first she just licensed her designs, but no one on Earth could imitate the Martian fabrics. So, even though it was fiendishly expensive, Marianne began exporting her creations to Earth where they became elite status symbols and then gradually evolved into expensive luxury clothes.

Marianne had to start training assistants to take over much of the orders, fittings, and sales business so that she could take the time to turn her ideas into new designs. She spent more and more time under her pink spotlight and on the surface.

She was now having genuine conversations with the natural forces in and on the planet. It wasn't like mere telepathic messages. Their "voices", for lack of a better word rang through her entire body.

"We like you," they said. "You are a welcome addition to our essence. We never paid much attention to quantifying time up until now, but as the planet cooled down, we must have retreated into a kind of hibernation. You say it has been billions of years."

"Well, who's counting," Marianne answered. It was convenient and pleasant that they now knew her, knew what she was thinking even before she consciously formulated her thoughts. She felt completely joined with them, the natural forces of Mars. It was her attempts at connecting with them that had activated them, for which they were grateful.

However, the forces didn't understand the human mortal creatures. They had just begun to notice them on the planet and considered them an itch they felt the urge to scratch.

Marianne set herself the new task of protecting her mortal customers and perhaps improving communication with the natural forces. She got the forces to consider the situation to be something allowing for more than one interpretation. They could regard the annoying mortal creatures as amusing and entertaining, and therefore harmless. After a fair amount of persuasion on her part, the Martian natural powers were open to this idea.

Marianne wasn't sure why, but she didn't tell the coven about her now complete connection to the natural sources of magic on Mars. She was apprehensive about what they would do with this information, and, frankly, she wanted things to stay the way they were. She didn't want to share her connection to the planet with her coven.

She and the Martian natural powers were now communicating beautifully. She told them about the witches and covens on Earth and why they had sent her to Mars. The Martian powers were surprised at the descriptions, especially that sources of magic on Earth functioned so chaotically and that Earth creatures who connected with this magic abused the powers they controlled rather than sharing them.

Then Ulrika announced that she was coming to Mars to take over the project and harness the magic forces on Mars for the coven.

Marianne decided to take a walk out on the surface to see if that helped her come up with ideas of how to deal with this annoying development. Just when things were going so well, Urika was hell-bent on ruining everything. Marianne gazed up at Phobos loping across the dusty, orange sky and fantasized about flinging Ulrika's rocket back to Earth before it even touched down.

Lost in thought, she disobeyed the first rule of surface strolling. She didn't pay attention to where her feet were going, slipped, and fell into a deep crevice.

Witches were more or less immortal, but their bodies could and often did sustain painful and debilitating injuries. Without thinking, Marianne switched to her magic mode to elevate herself out of the crevice before she hit any rocks.

Whoa! Suddenly she was flying over Olympus Mons, surrounded by a cloud of pink dust. Her magic never had that much power before. She had to get back to her apartment and rest before her reserves gave out. Funny that she didn't feel at all exhausted.

She hoped she slipped back into her apartment unnoticed, having first transported herself back to the habitat — that didn't tire her out either — and then entered the ordinary outside habitat door. Her robot vehicle — she now owned one — took her home.

Out of curiosity she used her magic powers to exit her surface suit and put on her favorite pink leisure sweatpants and shirt. After all the surface activity, she shouldn't have had any power left at all, but her magic worked instantaneously.

Instinctively she turned on the pink spotlight and entered her circle. She connected with the powers of Mars immediately. "Hey, can you tell me what is going on?" she thought toward the powers of the planet.

Now that she had activated them, they were capable of acting much faster than in their hibernation state. "Sure, why not?" they answered. "Good thing you decided to use your strengthened powers."

"But how did that happen?" she asked.

"You know," they began. "We've been registering your unhappy feelings after you conversation with your coven. We then decided to link up with the natural powers on Earth to learn about the situation there."

"The natural forces on Earth are an interesting bunch and of course had no idea that we exist. We've enjoyed some fascinating conversations. It was a surprise to find genuine kindred spirits on another planet. We should have searched for them sooner."

"Well, you have plenty of time now," Marianne said. "What do you make of your different situations?"

"We are slow but thoughtful," the Martian magic powers answered. "And our Earth colleagues are chaotic and spontaneous, a fun bunch, but they also make us a little nervous. Still, we have a lot in common."

"And where is this new connection going then?" Marianne asked.

"We've had several quite productive dialogues," the Martian powers transmitted. "Our Earth comrades preferred to maintain their chaotic state, and we plan to remain slow but steady. However, we would definitely join forces when circumstances demand, like when the sun gets ready to go nova."

"Interestingly enough, however, they recognized a definite advantage to being much more selective about which mortal life forms they allow to connect with them. Many such creatures just drain away Earth natural powers for their personal gain."

"Our Earth associates have decided to first disconnect all mortals and then reconnect them on an individual basis, after each separate mortal creature had proven itself worthy."

"We immediately saw the wisdom in this and decided to give you complete access to all magic powers of Mars."

"That's why I could fly over Olympus Mons so easily and not experience any loss of power," Marianne said. "I'm going to have to get used to this."

"We want you to have the necessary peace of mind for your future activities here," the Mars forces continued. "We hope we can continue our profitable cooperation. You need give no further thought to this Ulrika creature who kept upsetting you. The Earth forces have taken away her magic and she will have other problems to deal with besides selfish jaunts to Mars."

Marianne was overwhelmed with gratitude and joy, also happy that her new friends, the sources of magic on Mars, would be able to pick up on these feelings immediately.

Without even thinking, she spontaneously used her new powers to color her entire apartment bright pink, feeling the power bounce back and forth between her and her walls.

Now she had some really unusual new ideas for her Martian fashion designs.

REQUIEM FOR A GOBLIN

Lamont A. Turner

"It was raining the day they laid old Tye to rest. Blind, and hobbled by the gout, Tye hadn't been of much use to anyone, not even himself, for years, but he told the best stories. Some people used to say he was a prophet and he wasn't really blind in the usual sort of way. They used to say he had a hard time making out what was happening in the present because he was seeing the whole past and the whole future all at once. I don't know how true that was, but I, like most of the kids in town, would gladly skip a swim in the pond, or an afternoon of stick ball to congregate at his feet on the porch of his cabin, listening to his tales of ghosts, ghouls and, most of all, the goblins he claimed haunted the woods surrounding the town. We used to joke that he knew so much about goblins because he was one himself, although a more benevolent one than his kin.

"The goblin people are all black, head to toe, cept a course the whites of their eyes, an their teeth," he would tell us, punctuating each sentence by taking a long draw on his pipe. "They hides in the shadows, wait'n ta snatch up girls an boys who disobey their elders, an they carry 'em off. They whisk 'em up into the trees, and drag 'em down into holes in the ground. Nobody ever sees 'em again."

This was unwelcome news considering most of us were disobeying our parents just by being there at Tye's cabin. They disapproved of the old man and the hold he had over us. Sometimes we would have nightmares, but we always wandered back to that cabin on warm summer afternoons to hear more about the ghosts that wail in the night out by the old Jenson house, and the little people who carried off children who were bad, of foolish enough to venture into their domain.

The muddy soil splashed back onto the overalls of the gravedigger as he patted at it with his shovel. Normally they would have waited until the weather cleared, putting Tye in the storage vault they used for when the ground was too frozen for digging, but everyone was anxious to get Tye in the ground after what had happened. There had been no funeral, and nobody stopped by to say any last words as they put Tye in what everyone hooped would be his final resting place. I was there though. I owed him that much.

As I stood there, watching the rain poke holes in the mud covering Tye, I thought back to that day fourteen years before when all the trouble had started. It had been raining that day too. It hadn't been a fresh, cleansing rain, but was, rather the culmination of several dreary weeks that had left the countryside a morass of mud and mosquitoes. I still remember how the air had been heavy with the scent of rotting wood, and the mold that had appeared to envelope the houses, staining the white siding of our home green and black.

On that particular day, those of us who had been willing to slough through the mud to reach Tye's cabin on the hillside were sitting on the porch, in a circle around Tye, as was the usual arrangement, but that day there were no stories. Tye just sat there, rocking in his chair, and staring out into the woods. I remember how we all followed his gaze, forgetting he was blind. As the drizzle turned into a downpour, he seemed to grow agitated, rocking faster to keep time with the patter on the tin roof, plumes of smoke billowing from his pipe.

"They'll be coming for me soon," he said, jolted from his silence as the wind threw droplets of rain into his face. "I want you children to promise me you all will stay out of the woods. This is a goblin rain. Ain't no good can come of it."

We all moved farther up on the porch to avoid the rain, and waited for the story we believed Tye had been setting up with this declaration, but he had lapsed back into a trance, his dead eyes focused on something out among the trees. The rain drops on his cheeks looked like tears.

Eventually the rain relented, and we crept back toward our homes, dissatisfied and bewildered. I planned to go back the next day, not so much to hear a story, but just to make sure Tye was alright, but as things turned out, I would never go back there again. None of us would.

The next morning the police were at my house. Sheriff Cranston and a few men in suits I didn't recognize were in the parlor, asking my mother if they could speak with me. I heard him tell her Becky Demaris hadn't made it home last night. Some of the other kids had said she had been with us at Tye's cabin, and they had already been up to talk with Tye, who claimed to know nothing of the girl's whereabouts. As I listened in the hallway as the sheriff talked about making preparations to drag the pond as soon as the storm let up, I knew they wouldn't find her there.

I told the sheriff Becky had been at the cabin, but that I hadn't paid much attention to her, which was true, and that I hadn't noticed where she was headed when we left, which wasn't. After the sheriff and the others had gone, my mother scolded me for going up to the cabin, and promised dire consequences if she caught me hanging around "that spooky old man " ever again.

They have a stone up for Becky not far from where they put Tye. Of course there isn't anybody under it, but Becky's parents still put flowers on that empty grave until they both were laid to rest in graves of their own, one on each side of Becky's. Most people said it was out of guilt for never showing much attention to Becky before she vanished, and that Becky's mom had never known how to handle her spirited daughter. Becky's parents had adopted the dark haired girl when they were themselves going gray, and keeping up with her presented a challenge they were not equipped to meet.

I could see the three graves, now barren and forgotten, from where I was standing. It was as forlorn a spot as one could imagine, but probably not nearly as grim as that place where Becky really was.

Just seven years old, Becky was the youngest member of Tye's congregation, and was seen mostly as a nuisance by the rest of us, our interaction with her being mostly limited to pulling on her pigtails and stealing the old rag doll she insisted on carrying around. She also lived on the other side of town, beyond the woods, and that was where I had seen her heading as the rest of us made our way down the hill toward the road.

I didn't tell the sheriff I called to her that day, reminding her of Ty's prediction. I didn't tell anyone how I had watched, with growing trepidation as she plodded on towards the woods, either not hearing, or choosing to ignore, my warning. As I watched the woods swallow her up, I ran after her until I reached the edge of the forest. I hesitated before the trees that reached up out of the ground to rake the sky, and form a barrier between the town and the looming darkness. Unsure what to do, I glanced back to see the other kids had already disappeared over the hillside. Standing at the mouth of the narrow path Becky had taken, I shouted for her to come back, but my only answer was the rustle of branches, flailing at the wind. As I stood there, my courage unequal to the demands of my conscience, a peal of thunder announced the heaven's hostile intent, and I soon found myself seeking shelter beneath the overreaching branches. The rain had decided my course.

The storm was fierce. As I made my way down the path, the wind howled around me, and the canopy of branches above failed to fully shield me from the downpour. At the edge of a clearing I paused at a spot where the intertwining branches above provided a modicum of shelter. It was then, looking out across the clearing, that I saw her. There in the center of that clearing stood Becky, seemingly oblivious to the rain pouring down upon her. She just stood there, her gaze transfixed on the trees in the distance. Through the rain I could just make out something moving along the line of trees beyond the clearing. There were at least four of them. Becky saw them too, but seemed frozen to the spot, able to do little other than whimper. As they crept closer I saw that they vaguely resembled men, but they were smaller, not much taller than the girl they were inching toward. Other than their size, and their ape like gait, I wasn't able to discern much, for the creatures were entirely black. Like shadows they enveloped Becky, and dragged her back with them into the forest. Her whimper grew into a scream that was cut off almost as soon as it started by a black hand over her mouth.

As I watched them disappear into the darkness, the rain abruptly stopped, and an unnatural stillness settled over the scene. I would have doubted any of it had been real had it not been for the rag doll, lying there in the otherwise empty clearing, a testament to Becky's passing.

They never found Becky, and I never told anyone about what I saw that day. Just like Tye said, they came for him not long after, and, though they could never prove he had anything to do with Becky's disappearance, they found an excuse to lock him away. I always wondered if it would have helped Tye if I had confessed what I knew, but I was young, and I was scared, and wanted nothing more to do with goblins or the police.

I stood there in the graveyard for several minutes after the grave diggers had tossed their shovels in the old white van, and drove away, then headed back to my car. Glancing back as I pulled onto the road, I thought I saw several shadowy figures emerge from behind the stones to make their way toward Tye's grave. I could have sworn one of them, smaller than the others, had pigtails. I quickly turned away, and kept my eyes on the road ahead the rest of the way home.

THE FIFTH STAGE OF GRIEF

Cedrick May

Daniel peeked through the dining room window at his friend standing on his front doorstep, making sure not to make a sound as he slid the venetian blinds apart with careful fingers. His friend, Roderick, reached up and rang the doorbell for a fourth time. He then planted his feet, bowed his head and clasped his hands behind his back—he was determined to remain at the door for however long it took.

Daniel let the blinds fall back together. He stepped around the corner into the narrow foyer and opened the front door.

Despite his seeming knowledge of Daniel's presence in the house, Roderick looked a little surprised when he saw his friend. Or, perhaps, it was Daniel's appearance. It was 1:00pm on a

Wednesday and Daniel was still in his pajamas. He had lost a lot of weight. Daniel gave his friend a smile that looked more like pain than joy.

"Hi, Rod." Daniel looked at his watch. "Is it a holiday, or something? You should be at work, right?"

"I took a long lunch so I could swing by." Roderick started to say more but hesitated. He shifted his weight, pondering his next words. He ran the palm of his hand over his short-cropped hair. "We're all worried about you, man."

"I'm fine," Daniel said, widening his pained smile as he rocked nervously from one foot to the other.

They stood in awkward silence.

"May I come in?"

Daniel snapped out of his malaise, apologizing to Roderick as he opened the door wide. Roderick stepped through the doorway, looking around. Everything seemed okay, except for the quiet, except for a palpable emptiness that permeated the air. Roderick's footsteps echoed on the hardwood floor as he stepped in.

"You don't return calls anymore, bud," he said to Daniel who was still standing slump-shouldered in the open doorway.

"I'm sorry. I'm still... adjusting." Daniel absently fiddled with his gold wedding ring, twisting it between his right thumb and forefinger. "I'm, uh... just not up to coming back to work yet--"

"I'm not just talking about work."

"Sorry. I'm just not up to doing much at all, really."

"We all miss Emma. We miss you, too, D."

Daniel barely registered his friend's remarks. He gave a noncommittal nod.

Roderick took a flyer from his jacket and gave it to Daniel. It had information on it for a grief counselor. Daniel looked up at Roderick for the first time, surprised.

"You need help, D. You should go see her."

"I don't want to forget her, Rod."

"It's not about forgetting," Roderick said, pointing at the flyer in his friend's hand, "You need this, okay?"

Daniel nodded again. "Thanks."

"I'll take you by force, if I have to," Roderick said with a gentle smile. The two friends hugged, Daniel promising to give the therapist a call.

Daniel closed the door behind Roderick then looked at the flyer, noting its mention of the five stages of grief and a promise from the therapist to help guide the bereaved through their feelings of loss. He dwelled for a while on the list of stages: Denial, Anger, Bargaining, Depression, Acceptance.

Acceptance.

Daniel frowned. The persistent, suffocating emptiness in his chest felt like a permanent condition.

Daniel saw a movement out of the corner of his eye, what looked like a shoulder rounding the corner to disappear into the living room. He crept to the edge of the foyer and peeked around the corner to find that no one was there.

Three months into therapy, Daniel was doing much better. He began seeing friends and being more sociable at work. After six months, the pressure in his chest was gone.

His friends began to remark to each other that he was almost the same person as before the accident--getting out, smiling a lot, exercising, doing most of the things he had always enjoyed doing. About this time, his friends started asking him about dating. He would smile a little and fiddle with the wedding ring he still wore. He told them he wasn't quite ready for that yet.

Fourteen months after the accident, Roderick introduced Daniel to a friend who was visiting from out of town. She was thinking of relocating and Roderick asked Daniel to show her around. They hit it off well the first night, and she asked Daniel if she could see him again. They agreed to dinner the night before her flight home.

After the restaurant, they decided to spend more time together at his house. "What would you like to drink?" Daniel asked Pauline as they entered the kitchen.

"Whatever you have," Pauline said, throwing him a bright smile.

Daniel felt the chemistry between them on the first night. They drove around town all that afternoon, Daniel acting as Pauline's tour guide, laughing and trading horror stories about moving the whole while. Tonight, however, at dinner, Pauline asked Daniel about the ring he still wore. He knew Roderick had told Pauline about his situation, about Emma. When Daniel began talking about his wife, that she had died in a car accident, Pauline listened very graciously, giving Daniel time to reflect. Daniel's therapist had warned him in recent sessions, should he find himself on a date, to be careful not to do that. She suggested he think of and practice conversation starters that did not involve her in the event a dating conversation began to lag. But the conversation with Pauline never did lag, and everything felt natural with her, even his talking about Emma. Eventually, they segued on to other topics that had them both chuckling and enjoying each other's company again.

Daniel took in Pauline's smile as he reached for the refrigerator door, "I have some Rolling Rock," he chuckled, "hope that's okay."

"That'll be just fine," Pauline laughed as she leaned back against the countertop.

Daniel turned, opening the refrigerator door, then screamed. He leaped back several steps and banged his back against the adjacent wall, eyes wide with terror as he stared into the fridge.

Pauline immediately crouched into a fight-or-flight stance as she screamed out, herself, startled by Daniel's sudden outcry.

"What is it, Daniel? What's wrong!" Pauline called out, her heart in her throat.

Daniel gaped, speechless, into the refrigerator. Pauline could see him working his jaw as if trying to say words that would not come, trembling.

"Daniel?" Pauline took a tentative step forward. Her movement snapped Daniel out of his trance. He shot a glance at Pauline as she slowly leaned forward to peek into the refrigerator, to see what he was looking at.

Daniel leapt forward and slammed the door shut, startling Pauline again. He leaned with his shoulder against the door

"Don't come over here!" he shouted, pushing against the refrigerator until it started to tip backward, then slamming back down with a heavy rattle. "You have to go!"

"What the fuck is wrong? What's happening?" Pauline screamed, frightened tears forming in her eyes as she backed away from Daniel, wary of him now.

Daniel continued leaning against the refrigerator door, as if holding it at bay. "I'm sorry, I can't do this... you have to go."

Pauline just stared at him, unable to form words of her own, both frightened and gobsmacked. She could see Daniel was trembling uncontrollably now, and tears were flowing down his face. "I can take you back to the hotel," he offered.

Pauline waited on the curb outside Daniel's house nearly an hour for Roderick to arrive, jumping into his car as soon as he drove up to the curb. Daniel, watching from a window, could see her in the car talking with exaggerated hand gestures to his friend, terribly upset. Roderick gave her a hug and they drove away.

After watching Roderick's car disappear down the road, Daniel went back to the kitchen. He stared at the refrigerator for a long moment before stepping forward and gently pressing his ear against the door. He felt the cool metal of the stainless steel against the side of his face and the vibrations from the quietly-humming motor, but there was nothing else.

Steeling himself, Daniel braced one hand against the side of the refrigerator as he grasped the door handle with the other. He jerked the door open... and stared, surprised, as there was no sign of anything other than groceries and far too many half-eaten meals inside the box. Daniel relaxed and leaned against the frame of the refrigerator door, relived that what he *imagined* he saw was just a figment.

A sudden movement to his right caused Daniel to jump. He spun, alert again, but the darkened kitchen was empty. He walked slowly to the edge of the room and eased his hand around the corner, groping to find the light switch for the adjoining living room. He felt the familiar knub and flipped on the lights. Nothing. The room appeared to be empty.

Daniel sat on the edge of his bed with his face in his hands thinking about his wife, Emma, her mangled body lying stiff on the coroner's table. It was an image burned into his mind's eye. One side of her head was crushed and the other mutilated nearly beyond recognition by gaping lacerations. But he knew it was Emma. The medical examiner's office had done their best to make the body more presentable, but he hated them for making him look at her that way.

He was seeing her again now. Same as that morning at the coroners.

Roderick called later that night, angry and wondering what the hell had happened.

"What in the name of Jesus is wrong with you, man? You scared Pauline shitless!"

"I saw Emma..."

"Holy fuck, man..." Daniel could practically hear Roderick shaking his head on the other side of the line. "Look, I'll talk to you tomorrow. What you did was *not cool!*" Roderick ended the call before Daniel could say anything more.

Daniel went into the bathroom and picked up his wedding band from the folded towel next to the sink, where he had left it there earlier that evening. It was the first time he had removed it since Emma's death. He stared at it, then slid it onto his finger.

After that night with Pauline, Daniel began seeing glimpses of what he believed to be Emma's shadow with increasing frequency--darting around a corner in one place or another, just out of sight in the far distance elsewhere. He was always wound up, ready to spin at any moment to catch a glimpse of his wife. But that anticipation soured when he began seeing her directly--one body part at a time--at unexpected moments. Emma would appear to him as a pale, twisted leg inside of a cabinet; a wet, bloody arm under a counter; a glimpse of the left side of her face that had been crushed by the impact of the car collision, her left orbital shattered in a way that caused eye to bulge unnaturally from its socket. Emma was always catching him by surprise.

While taking out the garbage one morning, Daniel lifted the trash barrel lid to find Emma's whole body stuffed at the bottom of the bin, her face straining upward, mouth agape, eye bulging from its socket. He never allowed his gaze to wander into the bin again after that.

He once opened the silverware drawer to find her pale, water-soaked hand lying palm upward on top of the forks and spoons. It seemed to snake up from somewhere beneath the hollow space under the counter.

Daniel never opened the trunk of his car for any reason.

Over time, sightings of Emma became so frequent they became a normal part of Daniel's daily life. At that point, he had withdrawn from going out or spending time with friends again. He lapsed into a routine of work, home, work, home, with only occasional trips to the supermarket for groceries. Emma was there, too, gaping at him with her one bulging eye through the gap left between cans of soup, or the cold space left after pulling out the last half-gallon of milk from the freezer.

Daniel eventually built up the courage to tell his therapist what he was seeing. She suggested his date with Pauline may have triggered feelings of guilt that were compounded by his dwelling on the circumstances of his wife's death. She offered that these sighting--coupled with his insistence on continuing to wear his wedding ring--constituted an attempt to *bargain* with the deceased. She encouraged Daniel to reach out to his friends, to work out new routines, and try living as normal a life as possible--but to take his time, perhaps, with dating. She suggested group therapy, as well, so he could talk about his experiences and feelings with people who've gone through similar losses.

During a subsequent session, Daniel admitted that seeing his wife this way was beginning to feel normal, that, in a certain way, he kind of looked forward to them. The therapist told him she had reached the limits of what she could do for him and recommended he begin seeing a psychiatrist. She gave him a recommendation.

Daniel stopped going to therapy, altogether, after that.

With the end of therapy, Daniel withdrew further from his friends. Even Roderick stopped calling to check in on him. It seemed the frequency of Emma's visits began to decrease, though they didn't stop altogether. Now, in the times Daniel allowed his mind to wander away from his normal routine, she would appear, startling him again, but no longer invoking the same terror he felt the first night with Pauline. No, it was more like one of those ordinary moments when a person rounds a corner and nearly bumps into a spouse they forgot was in the house.

Early in the summer, Daniel noticed that a new courier was delivering mail at work. She would poke her head into his small office, where he worked as an actuary, to deliver packages. She was always beaming and seemed to relish her work as she dropped off the numerous envelopes, packages, and boxes that arrived daily.

"Good morning, Mr. Widner," she'd almost sing as she placed packages on the edge of his desk.

"Just Daniel," he would insist so she could ignore him and use his surname on her next visit.

Daniel enjoyed the courier's visits. Her nameplate read "Jeannie," and as much as she seemed to like her work it was also clearly hard labor as she pushed large dollies piled with deliveries up and down and in and out of the building, causing her brown uniform shirt to stick to her skin where the moisture collected on her back and neckline. Daniel could smell her sweat, an earthy scent that reminded him of Emma whenever she came home from a hard workout at the gym. It aroused him.

Daniel shot wary glances around his office, worried about what he might see hiding in the corner or filing drawer after one of Jeannie's deliveries.

One morning, the courier knocked on Daniel's door, announcing herself, as normal.

"Good morning, Mr. ..." Daniel raised an eyebrow and gave the courier a warning stare. "Ah! *Mr. Daniel*—is that it?" she chuckled as she plopped a thick envelope full of papers onto his desk.

"Close enough for now," Daniel said shaking his head. The courier left, pushing her loaded dolly past his office door and out of sight.

Daniel bowed his head, closed his eyes and took in a long, deep breath through his nose. He took in the smell of the courier's sweat, enjoying the arousal it brought on.

Daniel opened his eyes and sat up, looking around, prepared to see Emma draped in the corner or reaching from his filing drawer, but she didn't seem to be present. He settled in to get back to work when he noticed a small package on the floor in the doorway. He went over and picked it up, seeing that it wasn't for him. He looked down the hallway, searching for the courier, figuring the box must have fallen off her cart as she pushed by.

The box was addressed to someone on another floor and Daniel thought about delivering it, himself. He abandoned that idea as he stepped into the hallway.

Finding the courier wasn't on his floor, he decided she was probably traveling from top level to bottom, so he went to the next floor down, and the next, searching without success. *Shit! Maybe she was going up, rather than down,* he thought to himself. But he was already committed and kept going down, floor by floor, searching for the courier so he could return the package, thinking about her smell.

He finally landed in the lobby where he saw the courier exiting through the side delivery doors, pushing her empty dolly toward the delivery truck. Daniel called out as he ran to intercept her.

"Jeannie! Jeannie!" Daniel held the package over his head. The courier turned and saw him jogging toward her. He stopped and handed her the package. "I think this fell off your cart when you were going by my office."

The courier took the package and smiled, "Thank you, Daniel." A small jolt of electricity flowed down Daniel's legs when she said his name. He smiled back.

The courier turned back to her dolly, folding it into an upright position as she got ready to lift it into the back of her truck.

"Um, Jeannie..." Daniel began. Jeannie turned and considered him, head slightly tilted.

"Um, I was, uhm..." The words caught in Daniel's throat.

"Uh, huh, yes," she said, "I'd love to."

Daniel stood stunned for a moment, then started searching his pockets for a pen and some paper.

Jeannie stepped close to him and took a sharpie from her breast pocket. She took him by the wrist and began writing a number on the back of his hand. She stopped after writing two digits when she noticed the ring on his finger. Her shoulders slumped and she looked up at Daniel with deep brown eyes containing a terrible disappointment.

Daniel realized at that moment that he would always lower his hands below the level of his desktop to hide his wedding band whenever Jeannie came to his office. It was a semi-unconscious reaction, so he had forgotten in his rush to intercept her.

Jeannie dropped Daniel's hand and turned away without a word, tucking the sharpie back into her breast pocket. Daniel stood quiet for a moment, staring as she finished adjusting some cargo in the back of her truck.

"My wife, she's passed..." Daniel called out, surprising himself.

Jeannie stopped and turned, considering him with a skeptical look.

Daniel swallowed hard. "She's passed. A while ago. I'm... I'm just not ready to take the ring off yet. I understand if that's not okay."

Jeannie looked back at Daniel for a long moment. After what seemed to Daniel an interminable amount of time, she came back, pulling out her sharpie. She took his arm and finished writing out a number on the back of his hand, then stepped back as she put her pen away.

"You had better be for real." Jeannie turned and grabbed the strap dangling from the bottom of the folding door of her truck. She slammed the portal closed and set the security lock with a hard thrust of her palm against the metal bar. "You'd better be for damn real."

Jeannie picked up the small package she had set on the bumper of her truck and walked back toward the entrance of the building. She shot a glance over her shoulder at Daniel, looking him up and down as she disappeared through the glass doors.

Daniel stared at the number on the back of his hand with an excitement he hadn't felt in a long time. At that very moment a cold, wet hand slid across the back of his neck, causing him to spin around.

There were plenty of passersby, but no one who was within arm's reach of him.

Daniel and Jeannie met at a downtown restaurant overlooking the bay. Jeannie was already seated when Daniel arrived. She stood to greet him with a kiss on the cheek and Daniel was a little bit disappointed that she smelled sweet with the scent of a perfume he did not recognize.

They settled into conversation before the waiter brought them their drinks. By the time he returned to take their food order, they were deep into an animated discussion about the season finale of a television drama they shared in common. The frustrated waiter had to return three times before they were finally ready to order.

After ordering, Daniel excused himself to go the bathroom. On his return, he saw Emma was sitting in his chair across from Jeannie, head lolled to the side, eye bulging from its socket. Her long, wet hair hung in strings off the back of the chair, dripping water from the storm that had been raging on the night of her crash. The water dripping from her hair created a pool on the floor beneath the table.

Daniel felt his heart beating in his ears as he stood there, frozen, while Jeannie casually glanced over the drink menu.

"Sir, do you need anything?" a waitress asked, startling Daniel out of his trance.

Daniel shook his head, "I'm fine." He continued toward his table with uncertain half-steps, not knowing what to do when he got there. When he finally arrived at his seat, he stared, shaking, at his wife's sopping corpse.

Jeannie looked up at him and smiled. "Is this your wife?"

Daniel jumped, catching the attention of several nearby diners who gave the couple disapproving stares. Daniel gawked at Jeannie, then back at the corpse. "You can see her?"

"Uh, huh," Jeannie nodded, "Here, sit next to me," she motioned, pushing one of the extra side chairs away from the table a bit.

Daniel gaped at Jeannie, then the corpse, back and forth until he found himself sitting, staring in astonishment at Jeannie.

"I lost my son about ten years ago," Jeannie began, "I used to see him a lot, too. He'd show up at the most unexpected moments." Without realizing it, Daniel gripped the table, as if bracing himself. Jeannie put her hand on his and gave a gentle squeeze. "I can see you haven't gotten used to seeing her this way," she said, glancing back at Emma, "Looks like a terrible accident."

Daniel dropped his eyes to the table, "It was... a little over a year ago ..." He didn't know what else to say.

Jeannie looked around the restaurant. "Why don't we go somewhere else--I only live a few blocks away. We could pick up some Chinese." She gave Daniel's hand a little tug. "It's a bit strange, us sitting here staring at an empty chair and whispering in the middle of a restaurant."

"I had a feeling your wife might show up when you told me she had passed, so I was pretty much ready for anything tonight."

Daniel and Jeannie sat on the couch in her downtown apartment, mostly ignoring the takeout that sat cooling on the coffee table. Jennie told Daniel on the way over that her son had died from a gunshot wound suffered during a school shooting. She said it wasn't long afterward she started seeing him as he was when she identified the body. She told how she wanted so very badly to talk to her husband, Anthony, about their son and her "visions," but that he wasn't able to talk about what happened, that his grieving process was to suffer in silence and try to move on. "But *I* wasn't ready to move on," Jeannie explained, "I needed to grieve with someone, but my husband just couldn't bear talking about it..." Jeannie lowered her head and stared at the cold takeout in the table. "I can understand, to an extent, but..." She said, her voice trailing to a whisper.

Daniel reached out and took Jeannie's hand and squeezed it the way she did his at the restaurant. "How long was it before you stopped seeing your son?" Almost as a reflex to his own question, he began scanning the room with his eyes, expecting Emma to show up at any moment. Embarrassment at the selfish intent of his question washed over him when he saw Jeannie had noticed him scrutinizing the room. She just smiled, though.

"I still see him from time to time. Not in a bad way, mind you, but I do see him from time to time." Jeannie stood up and went to the mantle. She picked up a photograph and brought it back to the couch. "This is my Daevon," she said, holding the framed picture out to Daniel. He saw Jeannie with her strong brown arms wrapped around a bright-eyed little boy, about five or six years old. Both he and Jeannie were grinning for the camera, enjoying what appeared to be a kiddie park ride together.

"He looks just like you."

"Yeah," Jeannie said, looking with adoration at the photograph. "How about you? You have any pictures?"

Daniel took out his wallet and showed Jeannie a picture of him and Emma standing on a beach with their backs to the ocean. "We took this in Florida, about three years ago."

"She's beautiful," Jeannie said.

Daniel began to weep. Deep hard sobs shook him. Jeannie sat the pictures aside on the table and took his hands in hers again.

"Look at me," Daniel grumbled, wiping his face, "my therapist told me I shouldn't talk about my wife when I'm on a date."

"Well, she *did* invite herself along," Jeanine said, making Daniel laugh-cry at her gallows humor.

"How do you do it?" he asked. "I mean, no one else ever sees Emma when she appears to me."

"I don't know. While I was going through the divorce, I attended a grief therapy group. I didn't realize it at first, but it occurred to me at one meeting there were people in attendance who weren't, well... alive. And then there was a time when I went out with this one cute guy from the group and he freaked out when I told him I could see his dead wife in the theater with us. I even told him what she was wearing the day she died, and boy!" Jeannie laughed, "did he get the hell out of there quick! Never came back from getting a popcorn refill."

Daniel and Jeannie laughed.

At that moment, Daniel saw a shadow on the floor dart by. He shot a glance at an open door.

Jeannie followed his gaze. "She's here now, isn't she?"

"I'm not sure."

Daniel watched as Jeannie stood and went to the open door leading deeper into her apartment. She reached in and flipped on a light, sticking her head in to look around, then switched it off again. She turned and gave Daniel a little shrug. "No one here."

A pale, wet hand emerged from the dark room behind Jeannie, reaching for her. Stale water slid off the waxy flesh, making small splashes on the floor.

"Jeannie!" Daniel jumped from his seat to run to her, but Jeannie, seeing his panicked expression, held up a restraining hand and shook her head. Daniel stopped in his tracks.

"It's guilt, Daniel." The long, wet arm snaked from around the dark corner until Emma's hand rested on Jeannie's shoulder. "Your eyes tell me she's here, but it's guilt that brings her on." Daniel watched in horror as Jeannie's shoulder became soaked in dank water that filtered down the front of her blouse, causing it to cling to her skin. She winced with a slight shiver at the seeming uncomfortable chill of the filthy water.

"Jeannie..."

"No, Daniel..." she said with firm resolve as Emma's wet sinewy hand slid up her shoulder. "You have to replace that feeling with something else." Daniel saw the crusty remains of the neon green polish Emma used to wear on her blackened fingernails. Her long fingers wrapped into a loose hold around the front of Jeannie's throat, a filthy index finger gently stoked her neck.

"Can she hurt you?" Daniel said, fighting the urge to leap forward and rip away the hand on Jeannie's throat.

"I don't know."

Daniel closed his eyes. Breathing hard, he gripped his hands into tight fists, his body shaking. When he opened his eyes again, he saw Emma's other arm was now wrapped around Jeannie's waist. At that moment, he imagined Jeannie being pulled into the darkness of the room at her back, that she might disappear into the gloom.

Daniel rushed forward and took Jeannie by the waist, pulling her to him, kissing her with an even mixture of fear and desire. When Jeannie returned the kiss, leaning into him, he wrapped his arms around her and held on tight. They commanded each other's passions like that a long time, lips caressing, tongues probing, hungry.

The pale, cadaverous hand and arms slid from around Jeannie's neck and body and stole back into the darkness.

"Daevon didn't want to go to school the day he died, said he felt sick." Daniel and Jeannie sat on the couch now, Daniel with his arm around Jeannie's shoulders (that Daniel had been surprised to find completely dry) while she held his hand, running her thumb over his palm in a way that tickled a bit but gave him calm. "But he wasn't running a temperature, and I didn't see anything wrong with his throat. I watched Daevon get on the bus, and..." Jeannie clapped her hands together, making a loud *pop*, "that was the last time I saw my little boy alive. I was eaten up with guilt for *years*. Jeannie took Daniel's hand in hers again. "I think Anthony carried a lot of anger at me for what happened. It wasn't until I started to forgive myself that I stopped seeing him the way he was on the coroner's slab."

"But you still see him?"

"From time to time. But it's different now."

There was a long silence. Daniel could hear the muffled sounds of mid-town traffic filtering in though the living room window, the intermittent honking, an engine growling for attention as if the adolescent effort weren't mundane, the siren of an emergency vehicle pining.

"Emma and I had a fight the night she died. About money, about having a kid. I told her we weren't ready, and she told me *I* would never be ready, that I'd never be ready because I'm too... chicken-shit." Daniel paused, still watching Jeannie's brown thumbs stroking the palm of his hand.

"She was really angry, huh?"

Daniel nodded, "*That* was our tenth anniversary..." Daniel's voice cracked as he worked through the words. "Things got pretty bad from there. I wasn't listening... I made her so mad she tore off in the car during a storm to get away from me... I see her all the time now. I *think* about her all the time. I have to or..."

"Is she here now?" Jeannie asked, looking around.

"I don't think so," Daniel said, sneaking a tentative scan of the room. "Maybe."

Jeannie leaned her head up and kissed him.

"How about now?"

Daniel smiled and leaned down to kiss Jeannie without bothering to check.

Daniel held Jeannie by the waist as they stood in the open doorway leading out into the complex stairwell. "I'd like to see you again."

"Do we have any choice, Mr. Widner?" Jeannie said using her "office voice" and tossing her head to the side with a grin.

"You have to stop that!"

"You're cute when you blush," Jeannie teased. She pecked him on the lips. "I'll see you at the office."

"I can't wait!" Daniel smiled at Jeannie through the crack in the door as she edged it shut. She smirked back until the door was completely closed.

Daniel strode down the stairs of Jeannie's apartment complex with his mind reeling over the events of their evening together. His thoughts drifted to Jeannie's soft lips on his, her hands in his, her scent...

The sound of heavy footsteps running up the stairs caught Daniel's attention. He turned to find no one there, the sound suddenly gone. Daniel wondered if he had even heard anything in the first place. He craned his neck to look up the stairwell at the door of Jeannie's apartment. No one around. Daniel relaxed with a relieved smile and continued down the stairwell.

Jeannie stood in the kitchen putting away the leftover Chinese takeout in her refrigerator. As she arranged the soggy paper boxes on a shelf, she heard what sounded like claws scraping the floor behind her followed by deep-throated, watery heaving on the other side of the kitchen.

Peering around the open refrigerator door, Jeannie saw a slouching silhouette crouched beneath the kitchen table. Its eyes were like a pair of tiny bright lights staring out at Jeannie from the shadows. The thing beneath the table swayed from side to side, coiled, ready to spring. Its side-to-side movements creaked like old floorboards straining beneath the slow steps of a heavy man.

"I told you in the restaurant, you're not the first ghost I've ever seen," Jeannie said as she stepped away from the refrigerator. She kept her hand on the handle of the open door as she stared down at the murky silhouette.

The thing beneath the table gurgled and slid one arm slowly into the light from beneath the table toward Jeannie, blood-stained water flowed down the long, pale arm into a swirling pool on the hardwood floor. The thing leaned forward, creaking as it put weight on the exposed arm. Tangled locks of soaking-wet brown hair dropped down into the dim light, dripping more muddy water onto the floor. The bottom half of its mangled face came into view just below the shadow that hid the rest. It opened its jaws to reveal broken, jagged teeth. The glowing white eyes seemed to burn even brighter as the thing leaned forward, creaking like an old tree limb on the verge of breaking as it repositioned its legs to spring.

"I know what you are, and I'm not going anywhere," Jeannie said in a cool voice before jerking up hard on the refrigerator door handle, detaching it from the rest of the unit and holding it out toward the thing beneath the table. "All that anger's got nothing to do with me, take it somewhere else!"

The thing beneath the table arched its back and planted a hind foot, crouching in the shadow of the table on all four limbs now. It let out a long growl.

Jeannie gripped the refrigerator door handle with both hands, drawing it back.

"Oh, you're something special, aren't you?" Jeannie said under her breath.

The thing under the table slowly leaned its body forward revealing its distorted face from beneath the shadows, the torn flesh, the one empty eye socket drooling stagnant water, its bulging left eye askance as if looking off to the side somewhere--but Jeannie knew just where it was looking. Still growling, it crept one step forward. Its lead hand slammed to the floor sending out a spray of stale water from the dank slough that had collected on the floor beneath it. The impact of its hand boomed through the apartment, shaking the walls and causing Jeannie to jump with a start. She took a step backward, tightening her grip on the thick metal door handle, wringing it until the friction caused it to creak, then stepped forward again.

"Nuh, uh--not in my house!" Jeannie wound to strike as the thing under the table prepared its lunge.

A knock at the door caught Jeannie's attention and caused the thing under the table to turn toward the sound, its joints jerking like those of a startled marionette. Its neck arched outward like a curious animal as it crawled a step backward. Jeannie chanced a quick look towards the door, and when she looked back, the thing beneath the table was gone.

Jeannie lowered her weapon and went cautiously to the table and kneeled. She looked deep into the darkness beneath the table, then reached down to feel the floor with her hand. It was completely dry.

Jeannie sat back on her heels and let out a sigh. She looked through to the place on the couch where she and Daniel had been sitting earlier. "I sure hope you're worth this."

There was another knock at the door.

Jeannie opened the door to find Daniel standing in the hallway, a sheepish smile on his face.

"I just couldn't stop thinking about you."

"I know..." Jeannie took Daniel in her arms, holding him in a firm embrace.

"I just needed to see you one more time," he said. Jeannie nodded as she pressed her head against his chest. She could hear his heart beating fast.

"You're shaking," Daniel said as he nuzzled his cheek into her hair, "Everything okay?"

"Everything's fine now."

When they parted, Daniel noticed the refrigerator door handle Jeannie still gripped in her hand.

"What's that?" he asked pointing at the handle.

"Oh, the handle on my refrigerator door, uhm, it just fell off in my hand when I was, um... putting away the leftovers."

"I can fix that for you, if you like," Daniel offered with a smile. Jeannie laughed.

"Sure thing," she said grinning, "the tool kit is under the kitchen sink, handy man."

As much as they enjoyed each other, their histories made the couple ultimately decide to take things slow.

Daniel felt a delicious sense of anticipation for seeing Jeannie each day. At first, they tried to pretend everything was just as before at work, with Jeannie doing her regular "Mr. Widner" routine, but that quickly became a pretext for them to be flirty. Thursdays became the day Jeannie would "accidentally" drop a small package in Daniel's doorway causing him to have to chase her to the lobby to give it back and "save the day."

They laughed about their little office adventures on the weekends, but they spent most of their time going out, sight-seeing, taking long walks--doing things that allowed them to move around. Emma was still present, but much less often once they discovered she didn't show as much when they were moving around. Daniel and Jeannie tended to go on very active dates.

Daniel talked about Emma regularly, as did Jeannie about Daevon and her ex-husband. They often joked about the dating advice their former therapists used to give them.

"My therapist told me never to bring up Daevon, that it might scare guys away. I mean, he didn't say it that way *exactly,* but I got the message."

"Same here," Daniel said, slurping on a popsicle they were sharing as they sat on a park bench. "Mine said to keep it brief if she came up and then move on to other subjects. Like, '*Oh, my wife was killed in a tragic car accident--but hey, what do you think about the new Netflix pricing model? Think sponsored advertising will work?*'"

Jeannie giggled as she took the popsicle from Daniel for a turn at it.

As they sat in silence for a moment, Daniel looked across the jogging path at a group of small children romping all over the playground equipment. Parents either played along with their children or sat to the side staring absently into their cellphones while their kids dangled wildly from cringe-inducing heights.

Daniel tried to imagine what kind of parents he and Emma would have been. What would onlookers have seen? Would they have been attentive and participatory parents or phone-starers?

"Jeannie, you still see Daevon, right?"

"From time to time, yes."

"Since you see Emma when she's around, do you think I'll ever be able to see Daevon?"

Jeannie lowered the bright red popsicle from her lips, a look of surprise on her face. She stared quietly into Daniel's eyes as if searching for something in their depths. He worried he might have said something wrong, but then Jeannie's face softened. She put a hand on his cheek. Daniel saw tears forming in her eyes.

"Would you like to?" she asked in a whisper.

Daniel nodded.

Daniel and Jeannie made love for the first time that night, releasing themselves for each other in a way they had not with anyone for a long time, insensible to everything around them except the immediate sensations of their flesh and their breath and long-neglected needs.

They were not alone. Two ghosts inhabited the room with Daniel and Jeannie as they shed the remnants of once-unbearable grief in each other's embrace. One ghost had changed over time from something frightening to something... different, something protective and healing. That ghost put an embarrassed hand over its mouth to stifle a giggle and snuck silently from the room for a while.

The other ghost crept into Daniel's closet and closed the door with a pale, wet hand. It settled in one of the back corners and closed its pinpoint eyes. It knew that a time would come when some petty argument, some minor grievance, some uncertainty or unwarranted jealousy would reawaken it. Then it would have the fuel it needed to ease out once more.

But for now, acceptance.

For now, sleep.

THE MARINER

Jennifer Walker

Samantha waited until the end of winter break to tell her mother she wasn't going back to school. They sat at the palatial peninsula in her mother's new Tribeca condo with a small village of Thai take-out containers between them. Her mother found out Samantha wasn't going to do the prep courses, or take the LSAT, or shop around for law schools to apply to in the fall, and the room became so airless Samantha thought she would choke. When her mother did speak it was over the acerbic rip of plastic lids she sent scudding to the floor.

"You have got to be kidding me right now Sammy.

"Of all the stupid, idiotic things.

"You can't just drop out of school to what? Work on a tan? *Huh*!

"This is the most important semester! How're you going to get a good internship now?

"Tell me how!

"What's this going to look like on your law school application? You even think about that?

"What the hell's wrong with you!"

There was nothing wrong with Samantha. She loved the sea. She loved the thunder of the flapping sails above and the lurch of the hull below. She loved to fly across the water in the thrall of a gust, waves breaking over her face. She did not love classrooms, or studying, or the law. But she couldn't tell my mother that.

Instead she said, "I'm going to be a deckhand on the largest sailboat in the world."

This did not help. Pad Thai erupted over the Carrera marble and slid to the ground. If she had known it was her last conversation with her mother she might have tried harder. Not knowing she just picked up all the lids and the Pad Thai from the floor and left her mother to eat under the glare of her $4,000 pendant lights alone

As soon as Samantha boarded the Ancient Mariner everyone called her Sam. She'd worked hard in college to get away from Sammy and always introduced herself with her full name, like the witch, but no one asked. She was the newest crew member, coming on after the charter season already started, and the only female deckhand out of six. She was there to be told, not to tell.

At first she thought my mother was right and she'd done an idiotic thing. In school, at least, she knew what was expected of her. Now she was like a baby who couldn't even crawl. The other deckhands would have to show her two, sometimes three, times how to scrub the decks or cleat the lines or set the anchors or trim the sails. Their irritation when she didn't get it right, when she used the wrong cleanser, or didn't lock the lines, or fumbled with the ratchet block, felt physical and she found herself cowering a little, protective as they stood over her and watched. It didn't help that they constantly poked at her gender with false concern. Comments like, "if you can manage it alright," or "if it's not too heavy for you," were so equally galvanizing and disheartening she didn't have emotion left at the end of the day to even feel sorry for herself. She didn't even try to make friends.

That's what made it so strange when the other deckhands waved her into a dingy two weeks in on her first afternoon off. It also carried the chef and the six stews and was headed to a nearby beach on one of the dozen tiny uninhabited islands of the Bahamas. As they bumped along and beers were passed she was a silent third party to the bawdy flirtations of a crew bonded by their months at sea. If she forgot about herself the scene was warm and congenial, like a gathering of high school friends after a summer apart. She stared at the crystalline water to remember why she was there, and as they neared the island large schools of blue tang flashed as they turned away from the dinghy's sides and black striped sergeant majors weaved between them like thieves through a crowd.

On the beach they set up a bonfire and a volleyball net and then a deckhand shouted, "Skins versus shirts. Stews are skins!", and Samantha watched them laugh and laugh because, of course, all the stews were women. She hung back, her beer still full, until, again, the deckhands waved her over. The stews were already stripping down to their bikini tops and she froze, realizing in her surprise she wasn't wearing a bathing suit. But the deckhands wanted her to play with them so she kept her shirt on and when, after she passed the ball successfully a few times and then scored a couple points with spikes that sent the stews sprawling until sand plastered their chests, there was a sudden shift, a tilt of the frame. The bosun, Josh, clapped her shoulder. The lead deckhand, Tyler, gave her a high five. The first stew, Amber, yelled, "Nice Sam!", when she set a hard volley over the net and third stew Casey even flounced and giggled when she missed her serve. Sometime during those couple hours as the sun reached down to the water, and everything grew sharper, and longer, and more precious, Samantha became one of them. One of the crew. And while they waited for Chef's lobster boil and watched the starlight shining in every ripple of the sea, she finally felt like her mother was wrong. She was exactly where she was supposed to be.

It was Josh who told them about the tsunami over breakfast six weeks later. Their last charter had left generous tips and everyone was still too blurry eyed from a night out in Bridgetown to even see their phones.

"It was a 9.9 earthquake," he read, his hand shaking as he scrolled down his screen. "There wasn't enough time…"

When he couldn't go on Casey continued. She read off the internet in a flat tone, the high register of her voice making a tasteless joke of the words. The entire eastern seaboard was gone. Portland, Boston, Providence, Stamford, New York, Jersey City, Philadelphia, Wilmington, Baltimore, DC, Richmond, Charlotte, Charleston, Atlanta, Miami. Washed away in a single night. No more pendant lights, no more kitchen peninsula, no more mom. Casey hadn't finished reading before everyone got up from the galley table and started to roam the boat, zombie faces lit in the hypnotic glow of their phones.

When Samantha looked up again she was midship, her back against a stanchion. They were anchored in the bay and the glare off the sea and sky hurt her eyes. The boat lulled in the light breeze. The masts stretched too high above to see their tops but she still searched for them as if, if she tried hard enough, they could be found.

After that things happened quickly. Russia and China invaded the US and took control of everything left east of the Alleghenies. The crew followed the war for as long as their phone service held out and then on the radio. There was fighting soon across Europe, Africa, and Asia as everyone took a side and their anchorage became fraught because of the heavy

Chinese investment in Barbados. Not able to reach the owners the captain decided to take the boat back out to sea. Samantha walked in on Amber trying to call the remaining scheduled charters, her face earnest and concerned as if she really thought she'd reach any of them and that, with the world upside down, they'd care. When she finally did reach a guest from Chicago and used that carefully measured, professional pleasantness to tell them the Ancient Mariner, due to unforeseen circumstances, would have to cancel their trip, it was like watching a mime swim a length in an empty pool. When she hung up she even turned to Samantha and said, "She was really nice about the whole thing, really understanding."

The day after the captain decided to stop flying the American flag the crew woke up to find the lifeboat and dinghy gone. The captain, the engineers, and Amber were also gone, as well as three quarters of the remaining provisions.

"Who's going to steer this thing?" Chef raged as the remaining crew huddled in the ransacked galley. "What're we going to eat? Those bastards!"

He broke down and cried then. He was a solid man, loud and extravagant in everything he did. But the crying was indecent. Everyone watched him with faces so hollow and tense they might have been skulls already.

"Come on guys," Sam said suddenly. She even stood up. "We'll be fine. We can fish. We've got plenty of gear on board for the charters. We'll drain the hot tub and fill it with rainwater. We've got plenty of buckets. We have solar. I know how to sail. And so does Josh, and Tyler, and the rest of the deckhands. This thing is so high-tech it basically sails itself."

She didn't know why she spoke up. It should have been the bosun or the second stew or everyone else who outranked her. But she had to let them know despite everything they still had the sun and the sea and they could live forever on those riches.

"You're right. Sam's right." Josh nodded toward her and slowly the others started to nod along. Like a gas leak purpose filled the galley.

"Yeah," Casey said, and her voice almost had its usual lift. "And things will get better, you know. And then those guys can come back and rescue us."

She was the first to kill herself. It was only a week later, four days after America fell to the new Sino-Russian regime, two days after the boat stopped getting radio transmissions in English. She'd downed a handful of Ambien with the last bottle of Belvedere. Even after he'd heaved her body overboard all Chef could talk about was the waste of good vodka.

Sam tried to keep the crew's spirits up the best she could by throwing herself into whatever task Josh assigned for the day. She was the first in the morning to check the fishing lines set out overnight and the last before bed to pour any condensation into the whirlpool water reserve. Chef drank more and more, and often in the middle of the day Sam found herself on deck adjusting sails or checking lines alone as the rest of the crew spent more and more time in their quarters. But they ate well. Their hauls of corvina, and snapper, and grouper never ended.

The second suicide was another stew and she jumped overboard one afternoon, naked, and swam directly away from the boat, right into the sun, until no one could see her anymore. Everyone watched in silence. The next morning they found Josh hanging from one of the giant masts. He left a note that said Sam was in charge. She thought the other deckhands and stews wouldn't like it, and was going to say it should be Tyler, but Chef came barreling out of the galley at that exact moment.

"Who took my Captain Crunch?" he shrieked.

Sam was the one who'd found the Captain Crunch hidden in the bottom drawer of the oven and shared it with the remaining deckhands and stews the night before. They'd sat in the downstairs lounge after Chef had gone to bed and passed the box like it contained cocaine, each taking a pinch or two and sending it on. But it was Tyler who said he did.

Chef's knife shimmered like heat distorted air before he plunged it in Tyler's throat. Then there was chaos. No one thought about Josh or cutting him down.

Everybody took a side, as if that was the natural process of things, the direction everything was headed no matter what. The stews stuck together and headed for the stern with Chef; Sam ran to the bow with the deckhands. Manically inspired she shouted, "shirts versus skins" but there was too much screaming to hear her.

It took the rest of the day for the deckhands to barricade themselves in the rooms of the bow. They had the master suites, the bridge, and the fishing gear. The stews and Chef had the lounges, the whirlpool, and the galley. So they fought. Within a week the boat was down to just Sam, one other deckhand, and the chef.

It was around this time Sam started seeing her mother. At first she'd been like a blur in the corner of Sam's eye, cheering her on just like she used to at her softball games, when Sam grabbed an oxygen tank and bashed in the head of the stew guarding the whirlpool. Then she started hovering in the background while Sam talked to the remaining deckhands, almost unnoticeable, but still intently monitoring how often Sam led the discussions. Then she was around all the time, standing clearly in front of Sam and saying things like, "You're a born leader, start acting like it.", or "You're smarter than this Sammy. If they all jumped off the Brooklyn Bridge would you?", or "Take control of this situation or it's going to take control of you!"

Usually Sam hated her advice but now she could see her mother was right. Especially when the last deckhand threw himself overboard when, in a heavy gust, Josh's body finally came detached from his head and splattered all over midship.

"What did I tell you?" her mother said as Sam tried to salvage as much of Josh as she could for bait. "A bunch of pathetic losers. You're so much better than any of them. Now you just have to get rid of that ridiculous chef and you'll win!'

It was her mother who found the Ritalin left by the captain on a forgotten shelf in the bridge. "There's nothing wrong with a little extra help," she said. "Everybody's doing it. Mama

Sapperstein even got her vet to give her a script. How do you think her idiot son got through Columbia? Now you'll be able to sneak up on that cook in his sleep. He's got to go to sleep sometime."

Sam waited with her mother, hoping she was right, trying to be patient. Since Josh's body fell she'd heard whimpers and wails coming from the stern all day and night. What was it about being at sea that drove men mad? By contrast Sam was only growing stronger, keener, more alive.

At last the crying stopped and after enough time passed, just to be sure, she started out across the Ancient Mariner with a boning knife in her teeth and a carving knife in each hand. Her mother was beside her all the way. As she slipped into the galley where Chef slept with his fallen face in his arms she heard her say, "I'm so proud of you Sammy. I really am."

THE MEN WITH GREEN FACES

Christian Riley

'It's been six months since my grandpa, Walter J. Montgomery, passed away. He died in his sleep at ninety-two, in the spare bedroom of my home, where he had been living for the past five years. I am just now in his old house, packing things up, making this process of his finale complete. Well, I'm not really *in* his house, actually. I'm sitting on the rocking chair right outside, on the front porch, taking a much-needed break.

I've got two items in my hands on this break of mine. A soon-to-be-opened bottle of Steelhead Ale that I've brought with me all the way from my home, in Humboldt County; and one simple photograph that I've just found in a drawer. The ale has a distinct flavor to it, and for anyone who knows beer the way I do, they'll tell you that within this flavor is a subtle richness all its own. It's likely, in fact, that if you were to discretely pour a glass of this ale for a fellow beverage connoisseur, one sip is all it would take for them to realize what they were drinking. But I've been staring at this photograph for an hour already, and as a marine sniper with twenty years of experience, there isn't a person alive who could convince me I've got shitty eyesight. Yet nonetheless...

Some things in life never change much. My grandpa's house is a one-bedroom cabin in the rugged mountains five miles north-east of Coeur d'Alene, Idaho. Other than a few loose floorboards, some rotted siding on the south side, and a cracked kitchen window, this place is still exactly how I remembered it for all those times I've been here. It's still surrounded by a grove of pine trees, and it still overlooks that small lake right there, just past the green grass and rickety dock in front of me. I saw a moose standing in a bed of reeds on the west-end of the lake just this morning. Probably the same one I saw five years ago, when I came up here to get my grandpa.

On that day, Grandpa had been sitting on this very rocking chair as I came walking up from my truck. He wore green overalls and leather work boots, as if he had just finished cutting some wood, or was about to. But on his head was his faded blue, tattered ball cap from the Ford Motor Company. Grandpa won that cap at some auto-rally when he was eighteen years old, and for the entirety of his life, he only wore it on special occasions. As I said, some things in life never change.

But then again, there's this photograph in my hand. And it's of something completely out of this world. And as much as my head keeps telling me I've up and gone insane, or that maybe the altitude of these mountains has affected my way of thinking, I know my eyes have never lied to me. I'm opening this beer now, because even though some things never change... some things obviously do. And when that which changes is your own sense of reality, well, let's just say alcohol knows how to help smooth things over during a moment like this.

The Viet Cong used to call Navy Seals "The men with green faces." They came up with this term on account that the Seals painted their faces in shades of green and brown, helping them to blend in with their environment. Before their whole world would get lit up in a classic ambush that rained a barrage of .223 rounds, and half a dozen Claymore mines, some of these Viet Cong undoubtedly spotted a few of those white, hungry eyes staring out from the framed tapestry of the surrounding jungle—the men with green faces. But I'll tell you right now that those Viet Cong were not the first ones to come up with that term. And that those Navy Seals, with their painted skin and predatory eyes, weren't the first ones to be called by such a name.

February 5th, Nineteen forty-five. The Battle of Hurtgen Forest, near the Belgian—German border. That's where my grandpa, and four other infantrymen from his platoon, had been rescued by what they too called "Men with green faces." On patrol, they had gotten lost and wound up deep behind enemy lines. In short order, Germans surrounded them. The winter coldness was bone-chilling and tore at the platoon's morale like shreds of steel grating over soft flesh. But they fought with desperation, believing as they did that surrender to the Nazi war machine would grant them a fate far worse than death.

And so they fought, and then they died. Mowed down by gunfire. Blown to bits by grenades. Stabbed with bayonets. Men of the U.S. 28th Infantry Division, my grandfather's platoon, were slaughtered in a fierce battle with the Germans somewhere in that thick, snow ridden Hurtgen Forest—all except for my grandpa, and those four other men.

No one believed their story, of course, when they were found two weeks later after the battle which had decimated most of them. Soldiers from the American Army, fellow brothers of that war, simply balked at the tale those five men spun, pertaining to how they survived the German onslaught. They were given over to doctors to check their bodies—and their minds. They were suggested to be mentally incapacitated, gone insane from the horror they had endured in the forest, and then swiftly sent home to spend the rest of the war in a cozy hospital.

But photos never lie.

A local European newspaper ran a story about my grandfather and those four other infantrymen. How they were found in a half-starved state of decrepit brokenness. And *where* they were found. To be precise—what had surrounded them: the ring of filleted bodies.

"How could we have done this?" my grandpa had explained to his commander, in defense of his outrageous allegory of how they had been rescued. And over the years of my life, I heard my grandpa's version of this story only three times—all by eavesdropping on a conversation between him and my father. But every time, Grandpa's story was always the same, and in complete collaboration with what the European newspaper had printed.

In the last moments of battle, as those Americans were being overrun by Germans, massacred by a dreadful blitzkrieg, all at once there came a deafening blare from a great horn in the sky above. It was so loud that every man, German and American alike, stood frozen on the battlefield in complete awe. And after the noise came the blinding white light.

"It was all in their hands," Grandpa would say. "The men with green faces dropped from gray clouds, their hands extended into razor-sharp blades... all four of them. Four hands, that is."

He explained what those creatures looked like and how they moved. Ten-foot tall. Bald green heads, enormous eyes with thick eyebrows, green faces with braided strands of purple facial hair, at least a foot long. And four lengthy arms, each wielding a terrible blade.

"They moved like insects—you know? Jittery, and hoppy-like." He said they also jumped really high, and really far. They danced around the battlefield and all the soldiers, like cats playing with dead mice. And then the Germans began to scream and shout, cursing obscenities in their native tongue while those things darted back and forth, slicing them up. Slicing them up real good, cutting and hacking, tearing apart human bodies, limb by limb. A mass butchery.

The newspaper ran the article, and the Army was outraged: *American soldiers saved from certain death by the Germans, thanks to "other-worldly" creatures with green faces, and four arms, and large bodies immune to German bullets, and German grenades, and German bayonets.* It went something like that.

But those photos were there in that article. How could those men have done that? How could those five Americans who were found half-starved, frozen from both cold and terror, able to not only defeat the German army of over five hundred soldiers but also mutilate their bodies in the fashion in which they were discovered? And then pile them high into a colossal ring?

There were three pictures in that article. One was of my grandpa, and those other four men sitting in the back of a truck, blankets wrapped around them, their faces hollow and thin. They had been shivering from cold and fear. You could see it past their smiles and in their eyes.

And then there was the picture of the ring of bodies. *"It gave us shelter from the snowstorms. Maybe that's why we stayed in there."* That was the statement taken from one infantryman, as quoted underneath the photograph. Over one-hundred feet in diameter, and ten feet high. Five-hundred German soldiers ripped to shreds and woven amongst each other to create a great, circular wall of grisly death.

And then a last picture: a close-up shot at the face of one German soldier. His ending had been nothing short of absolute terror. That, you could also see in his eyes, past his screaming face locked forever in a grim howl, because of a complete and sudden death.

"How could we have done this?" my grandpa insisted. And then they sent him away.

I'm a grown man. I've been in two wars, myself. Hell, I've even worked alongside men with green faces: the Navy Seals.

I've seen a lot in my life, but to tell the truth, I've never had much of an opinion about my grandpa's amazing story. Perhaps my mind has always been too afraid to confront the possibility that my father's dad was a raving lunatic. That he wasn't meant to endure the grim realities of war, and that he himself, along with those other guys, simply snapped.

Yet that doesn't explain how he survived what he did. Or how those Germans were killed and piled up like that. And now, as I sit here in this chair and stare at this photograph—this *fourth* picture, which should have been in that original article, goddamnit—I'm finding that maybe it's *me* who's turned into a raving lunatic. Maybe I'm the one who's gone insane, unable to cope with the grim realities of having my entire life filleted, then woven into a colossal ring of denial that my mind just can't seem to accept. Or won't accept.

I'm opening another bottle of Steelhead Ale, as I stare at this photograph once more. I'm seeing those creatures my grandpa talked about. They're standing out on a bleak field of snow, eyes off in the distance as if searching for something, or taking in a spectacular view from atop a mountain. I can see that they each have four arms, long and muscular. They've got thick eyebrows that frame huge eyes, and faces that might be green if this photo hadn't been taken in black and white. And their faces end in a trail of long facial hair, braided, like rope hanging from their jaws. They look as if they might stand a full ten-foot high... But that's just a guess.

These are the men that saved my grandpa and those other Americans. I know this now. These are the men who fell from a gray sky, like angels descended from heaven, only to deliver a fury of death upon five-hundred German soldiers. The same men who, after killing all those soldiers, used their razor-sharp blades to butcher them, and weave their bodies into a ring of death. These are the men with green faces, and yes, they are most definitely beings from another world. In fact, there's nothing in this photograph that would convince me otherwise. Not even the tattered ball cap stenciled with the words "Ford

Motor Company," placed on the bald head of the one standing in the foreground, his smiling eyes staring at the camera.

THIS IS NOT MY BUTTERFLY

Joseph Hirsch

Claire stood in the doorway, on the threshold, ready for the night. She knew she should just push on, leave the house. But she hung there, frozen, eyes roving from the blackness outside to Micah still in the house.

"Hey, bay..." she said, and waited for him to turn from the screen, though she knew it wouldn't happen. After the silence grew too thick, she spoke again. "I'm headed to the library to Sylvia Plath it with Jaar."

That didn't move him, either. He just kept typing, hunching even further in that white tee, which was wrinkled and covered with grease stains.

"They don't have an oven so you don't have to worry about me killing myself while I'm there." There was a time (most of the years they'd dated, and the first couple years of their marriage) where morbid humor had been a great bonding tool. No more.

She sighed. Then she turned, opened the heavy wooden door, closed it behind her, and walked out into the cold night. The stiletto heels on her boots clacked hard on the concrete, and she shivered, pulling herself closer within the billowing folds of her faux fur coat.

This coat was her favorite, ersatz ermine that gave all the silky warmth of the real thing with none of the guilt. Both chic and kitschy, it looked real enough at first glance, but on closer inspection no member of PETA would have seriously contemplated ruining it with paint.

She'd gotten it at discount from Dead Threads, back when she worked at the vintage clothing store. The same place where she met Micah. He'd been browsing for a bowling shirt to wear for his rockabilly band's debut later that night in a local tavern.

Back in the days when he still did things, when he'd fooled her, the world, and himself that he wasn't insane. Back when he'd used his computer for work. Before he just kept typing a string of nonsense, each of the beads strung along the line joined only in the simplest, most free-associational manner: *Baby, diapers, baby powder, crib, how-to-avoid-Shaken-Baby-Syndrome. Milk, Formula.*

An infantile abacus of the absurd.

She shuddered, retreated further within the shaggy billows of her coat.

Some of it's my fault.

The thought came as sudden and harsh as the gust of wind playing with the fur's grey pelts, but she stuffed it down back inside. She would save it for Jaar.

Quickly, prompted by the cold, she found her daisy yellow VW Bug parked at the curb.

She opened the car door, greeted by the familiar scent of old leather and pine musk wafting from a tree-shaped air freshener. Her breath appeared in front of her in icy gusts, and she shivered again.

Being cold beat being in the house with Micah, where the literal warmth offered no solace, only a weird, rank sense of contamination. Like something alive that shouldn't have been, mold unchecked in a shower's grouts, or a greenish fungus culture on a cheese slice left too long in the fridge.

Life, greedy to devour, grow bigger at the expense of other life.

But then again, wasn't all life like that, life at the expense of other life being part of the very definition of life itself?

There had to be a poem—at least one—lingering there in the question.

The library loomed from the hilltop, a redbrick trapezoid with large windows that spilled warm light onto the lawn. A group of young mothers and their children were visible through the main window, sprawled out on couches and comfy futons, sharing oversized books filled with colorful pictures. Some of the moms looked bushed and just finished with work, wearing seafoam-green scrubs or charcoal-pinstriped suits. Others wore unseasonably thin yoga pants or ballet leggings mismatched with baggy grey college sweatshirts or cable-knit sweaters.

A pang passed through Claire, a hurt different from the one she felt at home, a bit more intense than it was around Micah.

Tell it to Jarre, she thought, tough-loving herself in an internal voice that made it sound like *Tell it to the marines.*

She drove up the hill, the old Beetle's motor straining, until it reached the crest, and parked beneath the dense boughs of some oak trees. She got out of the car, let a small man with a mountain of books waddle past her, and went inside.

Library smells—the ozone of copying machines and old glue barely keeping together moldering books—filled her with a calm that perfused her whole body.

Alright, it wasn't a Paris salon, or smoky cafelike interzone where shady jazzmen with Borsellino hats smoked hash, but it was all the culture she could afford right now. And thankfully, her and Jarre's poems had scared away the rest of those who'd initially joined the poetry group advertised on the lobby's corkboard.

The blue rinsers who wrote with the same lack of passion they filled out their bingo cards had been the first to leave. They'd quit as Jarre's stanzas had grown less and less veiled in reference to his failed attempts to come out to his drill sergeant father as a teenager.

The formalists had fallen off next. They had expected to pick apart Robert Frost's poems like blind birds pecking at seed, and grew intimidated when the time finally came to write their own pieces. And the awkwardness of reading impersonal, derivative rhyming verse about changing seasons, family dogs from childhood, or picking apples felt anticlimactic contrasted against Jarre's tortured confessionals.

The rest quit for more prosaic reasons, scheduling conflicts and general laziness, shying away from the harder exercises like the villanelle and sestina.

Now only Claire and Jarre remained.

She walked into the Activities Room, bright with fluorescence that made her squint, the thin loop carpet smelling freshly vacuumed.

"I love that coat," Jarre said. "You look like a minx, or a gun moll."

Claire pulled the billowing folds of the coat closer around her, strutted the rest of the way to the table, embracing Jarre's view of her as a vamp. "It's falling apart."

"Frayed," Jarre said, standing and moving around Claire, as if, like a dutiful butler, he wished to ease the fur off her shoulders. Instead, he just stroked the tatty frazzles of the shedding pelt. "She's threadbare, like a priceless Turkish rug."

"I like that you gendered my coat as a 'her,'" Claire said, smiling for the first time since...well, since the last time they'd been in the library together.

"'La capa' is indeed a feminine noun in Spanish."

"Oh," she said, lifting her coat slowly off her shoulders so Jarre could continue to stroke its fabric as she disrobed. "Are we doing Federico García Lorca tonight?" She struck the tilde hard on *García,* licking her teeth with a Castilian flourish.

"It was 'five o'clock in the afternoon,' awhile back," Jarre said. He glanced at his gold watch to make sure he wasn't making a lie of the Lament for Ignacio Sánchez Mejías. "And we'd better get started before they close, and throw us and all the crotch goblins and their mothers out for the night." He returned to his side of the great white table flooded with harsh fluorescence. In front of him was his brown moleskin notebook, the same color as the duffel coat hung on the chair behind him.

He leaned forward so that all of his lithe muscles coiled beneath his shirt, and his large Adam's Apple bobbed.

Why did she still have to find him attractive after all these years? Why did she have to be the cliched, quintessential hag?

She sighed, and he misinterpreted the source of her exasperation. Or maybe not. Maybe he knew better than she did. He leaned closer, found her fingers with his, taking her hands in his own. Just like in the old days. He arched an eyebrow, a bit of sympathy in his eye, a touch of a catty curiosity, too, that made him as much of a cliché as her.

"He still doing it?" Jarre asked.

"More than ever." Claire shook her head, a look of wonder mixed with disgust written on her face. Slowly, she extricated her cold fingers from his warm hands. It couldn't have been pleasant for him to fondle her bony digits soaked through with the iciness of the outside world. Not when he had been in here warming himself for...how long?

She twisted his hand slightly, and glanced at his watch.

"I'm sorry," she said.

"For what?" Now both of Jarre's eyebrows lifted, did a little dance that made him smile and her laugh.

But then she groaned, writhed in her seat, unable to accept the joy he brought her, feeling unworthy of it. "For being late."

"We've got bigger problems," Jarre said.

"What?" She braced for it. She didn't want to talk about Micah and his ceaseless strange typing.

What if it was some kind of brain virus, though? And it was communicable? And in a simple matter of time the lines of the hemp paper in Jarre's notebook became filled with crazy freewriting scribbles on the same subject?

Poems about the bullnecked father barking orders to his shy, unathletic son becoming *onesie, crib, Gerber applesauce.*

She shivered again.

"Hey," Jarre said, snapping his fingers back and forth. "I said 'we've got bigger problems.'"

Claire blinked back to the moment, sat up straighter in her chair. "What?"

Jarre pointed at the empty space in front of her. "You forgot your notebook."

"Ugh." She brought her palms up so quickly and dropped her head with such dejection that brow meeting palm produced a loud slap. "Ouch," she said. Then, "I feel like a first-class heel." Her own book, bound in grosgrain leather, lay on the basketwork table next to the front door, at home. She'd forgotten it on the way out. "And I had a good one, too, in iambic pentameter, about a butterfly pupating from my vagina."

"Hmmm, imaginative. I envy you your creativity, to say nothing of the extra orifice your sex boasts."

"I assure you it's not all it's cracked up to be." Her hands searched his out again, a reflexive action, grasping as if for a port in a storm. "Mine's broken."

Jarre squirmed. Obviously he didn't want to talk about her fertility problems. And why should he? Whether or not she ever had a crotch goblin of her own was none of his concern, except that it might make her happier, for a time. Like when the kid was a child. But then later it would make her miserable. Like, say, when said-hypothetical child became a teenager.

"Maybe," Jarre said, and that he left space there meant he was hesitating, because she might not like what he was going to say. But he had no choice now but to continue. She was watching him, seeming to hold her breath and needing his words as a kind of permission to breathe again. "Maybe he's sort of automatic writing his own kind of poetry. And this is his way of dealing with your guys' fertility issues?"

"They're *my issues*," she said, her voice sounding more pouty than she wanted.

"You said his sperm were stupid."

Claire snorted a laugh. It was a crude sound, piglike, and it embarrassed her to let it loose in front of anyone but Jarre. "I didn't say that," Claire said. "The doctor said that. And even though they're stupid and swim in crazy ways, his boys are still swimmers. There's nothing wrong with their motility. 'Dumb sperm are brave sperm.' The doctor actually said that. 'They don't hesitate.'"

"I wonder what my sperm are like? I mean, how smart they are?" Jarre pulled a hand away from her palms to stroke his chin, doing an impromptu impression of Rodin's Thinker. He was good at concealing the smile if he thought feigning graveness would make the joke funnier.

Claire, however, knew him too well, and said, "You have the sperm of a poet," forcing him to release the tongue from his cheek, and smile. "Cocteau had the blood of one, but the seed of inspiration is yours."

"The Muse has granted me great motility. And did you know that in German, 'Samen,' means both literal seed, as from a flower, and sperm?"

"Maybe we should write a Dingsgedicht about it," Claire said, unable to mask the despondence any longer with more jokes.

The *clickety-clack, clickety-clack* steady typing of keys continued. She wondered if Micah had even paused tonight to use the bathroom.

She opened the door, and the already-loud sound grew into an unbearable, almost unholy din. No attention-starved child banging the bottom of a pot with a spoon could have been louder.

Maybe that was it. He wasn't just typing in searches related to babies. He was becoming one, devolving into an immature, highchair-bound (or swivel-chair bound) sessile ball of echolalic babbling need. The thought made her shudder, but, like a chill in a bout of nausea, it passed and a flash of anger overcame her.

Quickly she glanced over at the wickerwork table where her pebbled leather notebook filled with poems sat. It had been his fault that she had forgotten it.

She walked across the entryway carpet, then over the hardwood.

She walked to him where he sat typing.

"Micah?" Against her better judgment, and maybe even her will, she felt her eye drawn to the screen, where the cursor blinked and danced across white space.

Baby's first steps, plastic rattles, teething tools.

What the actual hell?

At least before he had been performing searches online. Sure, the idle shopping hadn't led him to buy anything, but his actions had yielded results. There was cause and effect. He would search for something and find it.

But now he was in an **MS-Word** document, just typing gibberish into empty virtual space.

"Micah..."

A greasy smell caught her attention and she crinkled her nose. It was coming from somewhere near the keyboard. She looked down, saw an empty can of pork and beans resting at the corner of the desk. Brownish streaks of sugar and pork fat coated the side of the tin, staining the wrapper.

So he had at least gotten up to eat.

"Micah, I can't do this anymore."

He stopped typing, for what seemed like the first time in months. Only he hadn't stopped to listen to her. He'd stopped to read his work, lifting his hands, tenting his pointer fingers and thumbs into guns. He almost seemed to be admiring what was written on the screen. As if it were anything but the same stream-of-consciousness, baby-related gibberish he'd been typing all along.

"I'm sorry, alright!" She backed up, pulled her coat off her shoulders, as if freeing her arms for a literal fight.

The coat fell to the floor and she stood in a blue button-up cardigan, half open to show the iron-on "8" of a burgundy hand-me-down raglan soccer jersey. "I'm sorry I can't have children! If you're angry, if you want to leave me, I understand. There's no reason you should have to suffer with me. I know you wanted kids. You obviously still do."

Micah resumed typing, clacking the keys even harder so that the keyboard lifted up and danced, rattling side to side like a household appliance levitated by poltergeists.

"GODDAMNIT MICAH! QUIT BEING A PASSIVE AGGRESSIVE ASSHOLE! TURN AROUND AND TALK TO ME!"

Her words hung in the air. She put her hand in front of her open mouth, eyes watering, bit her quivering lip.

Micah stopped typing again, although this time he turned in his swivel chair.

He stared at her, eyes vacant, wide, red-rimmed, deeply housed in dark sunken orbits.

"I want to thank you for being patient with me the last few months, Claire."

A smile spread across his face, hideously alive and at odds with the deadness of the empty eyes. He grinned until his teeth showed, remarkably white for someone who hadn't brushed them in weeks, if not months. "And the baby's ready."

"The baby?"

Maybe he had been brainstorming, researching, finding out about children in order to use his graphic design and programming background to 3D wire-sculpt and then build a virtual baby. Some kind of cooing, goo-goo ga-ga'ing AI with which they could interact.

The pixilated child would only make her pine worse for the real one she couldn't have, but it would still be a relief. And a meaningful gesture of some kind, an explanation for his emotional absence these last few months.

She waited for him to bring up the file, to confirm her hope.

Instead, he shoved himself aside from the computer, and pointed to the modem, set in an alcove shelf below the desk.

She looked, saw, gaped open-mouthed.

The cable leading into the back of the modem was slick, leathery, greasy as the bean can, charred black and shriveled in places.

Had he lit it on fire, let a lighter linger there until the rubber insulation had warped and fused into this strange knotwork?

Or maybe there'd been a power surge that caused it first to spark then melt?

No, that wasn't it.

The line pulsed with life, something like literal juice rather than electric current moving through its length. It even made sounds as it swelled and contracted, produced belches that resulted in a gaseous, flatulent wheeze that sputtered little wet flecks through the modem's airholes.

She continued to stare, stunned, at the slick and coiling intestinal length of living cord.

"What the hell is that?" she asked, pointing.

Micah smiled. "Congratulations."

The cord pulled itself free of the modem with a suctioning pop that released a splash of goop that quickly hit the wall. A yellowish-green mucilage exploded there, slid down the wallpaper like a slime mold or a rotten uncooked egg some prankster had chucked, and it smelled just as bad.

The same kind of rotted, spoiled yellow-green suet poured from the plughole in the modem, sieving out slowly like sausage from a grinder.

Then the coil stood up, danced on itself with a muscular tension suggesting it had a spine. The sinewy knot balanced, cobra coiled to strike, charmed from its straw basket by a soundless shinai.

Claire took a step back.

The thing was a pruned mass of slimy flesh, a strange uncircumcised, eyeless monster, and yet it seemed to stare at her. Or at least, she could feel it thinking. The thoughts were somehow broadcasting from the locus of its intelligence housed in the nubby rounded orb in which it tapered up top, in its approximation of a head.

She moved along the table, feeling her way against it. As soon as she could feel something besides the table's wooden edge behind her, she was going to turn and run. Out of this house and away from this nightmare.

The cord of dancing flesh seemed to hear her thoughts, or read them in a psychic link Claire couldn't help but establish with her fear. Only instead of striking for her, it slapped out for Micah. It wrapped, vinelike, spinning around his throat. His empty eyes became alert one last time, long enough to bulge and show fear, swell in the sockets while his face turned pink, then flushed deeper red.

"Hghn!"

The love she had once felt for him came back, and she rushed forward. But as she did the coil of viscous, infinitely wrinkled skin strained tighter around his throat. Micah's red face turned purple and his eyes swelled as if they might explode in their sockets, the whites spiderwebbed and bursting with bloodshot fissures. His windpipe yielded with a series of consecutive crunches. The first was soft as the cracking of peanut brittle, but was followed by a harsh sound like a branch snapped by two strong hands.

At last, he ceased to strain against the rope of wet living meat, going limp. The umbilicus eased off, sensing his ghost had passed. Then it raised up once more, moving in a sinuous motion that hypnotized even as it menaced, making her both want to run away and walk toward it.

But *run* remained stronger in the mind than *walk*.

All she'd have to do was *bolt* without giving the snake a chance to snag her like some living liana in a sentient jungle.

Behind them both the modem cracked, snapping apart, yielding like a walnut hull.

The snake turned away from her to look, and Claire's eyes couldn't help but follow.

What remained inside the modem was a curled form, tucked on itself and dripping with gouts of afterbirth and jellylike red placenta thick as frogspawn.

The little creature opened its mouth, revealing soft and wormy gumlines, empty of teeth, where thick, milk-white spit bubbles proliferated and popped in quick succession.

The snake flew toward the baby's hand with the speed of a filament going toward a magnet. Quickly it lassoed itself around the babe's cherubic arm into a tightly coiled rope.

The baby crawled from the shattered shell of the cracked modem, gripping the rope in pudgy, ill-defined fingers, a barely ambulatory infantile impression of a cowpoke.

It moved forward with limbs ringed in rolls of soft fat, rugose folds that swallowed up its kneecaps, hid its elbow joints beneath their pasty layers. Its head was roughly spherical, but creased at the top. As if the obstetrician had used something crude as salad tongs for the extraction and crumpled the fontanel in delivery. Its features were gnomish, scrunched, frozen in the lament of life's first moment, ripped from permanent food and warmth and cast into the vail of cold hunger, harsh lights.

It opened its mouth again, once more revealing the tiny black hole framed by the bright pink maw of slick, toothless gumline. The hole yawned, strained wider, as if for a cry. Finally the baby belly-moaned, shrieking so loudly that a wind tossed the curtains over the windows, their frilly lace forms dancing back and forth.

The empty bean can next to the computer fell to the floor with a clatter. The skin rope trembled like a penis in the throes of orgasm, shivering in its lassoed coil, almost cowering beneath the concertinaing soundwaves of screams. Micah, open-eyed and open-mouthed, stared up at the ceiling, a purple line of stipples tracing his neck already bruised and showing signs of livor mortis.

Cold air played against Claire's backside and she spun, ran for the door which the baby's screams had blown open. A slick, wet sound came from behind her, the familiar scurry-slither of the rope unlimbering for action.

She reached the door, tasted the cool night air, felt something warm and wet slide around her foot.

"No!"

It yanked her backward and she fell.

She turned as it pulled her, dug with her fingernails at its viscous skin so that the weird extra-long piece of prolapsed umbilicus split along its seams.

"You fucker!"

The outer integument continued yielding to her sharp nails, the thin layer of reddish skin breaking to show sinewy, serpentine muscle coursing beneath. It pulsed, throbbed, and flexed through the channel heretofore-hidden by the armored hide.

She lifted the cord, and it strained against her, yanking her back toward the baby, who waited, tottering on his new legs, for her to come to him.

If she could just pull the cord close enough to her mouth she could lock her teeth on it, no matter how foul it tasted. Then all of the rage and fear of these last few months could go from her jaws directly into the veiny cable. She would bite through it, snapping it along the length, run out into the cold freedom of a dark and waiting night. Run to Jarre.

"Grhah!" Claire heard herself grunt, and her straining muscles, already fatigued from the fight against the rope's implacable strength, finally gave out with a last shiver. She went limp, and the thing pulled her now where the baby commanded.

"No," she said, but the thing, as voiceless as it was eyeless, said *yes* with its motion, tugging until she found herself lying in the middle of the room. The door, only a few feet away, might as well have been in a distant galaxy.

The meat rope curlicued so that its top half became a kind of crooked question mark. Then, with one lashing strike, it slapped the front of her body, splitting her jeans along the seams, shredding her cardigan and tearing through her jersey. As it moved closer now she saw it was covered, like an undersea creature, in serried rows of drag denticles and slurping suction cups. They made its job easier as it sliced, sucked, bit through first cloth and fabric, then satin, careful not to cut her flesh, until she lay naked.

Tears spilled from her eyes, and she had the absurd thought that if she could only reach her notebook, show them both—baby and intestinal rope—they would understand.

This is not my butterfly.

"Micah," she shouted, "help!" But he only stared, mouth agape, a husk, a cocoon whose duty had been fulfilled, his part of the mating ritual complete. "Jarre," she said, and laughed bitterly. What the hell would he make of this?

The baby waddled forward, seeming to pass through six months of toddling and struggles to remain upright in as many steps. By the time he reached her pelvis, he could balance his cumbersome lump of a head on his soft shoulders, and control his bowlegged gait much better.

She looked at him, at the protruding gourd of his potbelly.

A wet woundlike fistula, shaped like a star, covered the circumference of his stomach, the bloody birthmark-shaped socket that once mated up with the cable.

He reached out with his baby-fat hand, its clenching fingers making Claire giggle a bit even as she cried. They were *cute*, the fingers.

There was another suctioning pop, like the one that accompanied the decoupling of the cable from the back of the modem. The fleshy rope locked in place on the baby's belly, mating its meaty length with the leathery rosette where the infant's navel should have been.

The other end of the line, the dancing one, had ceased to slice with the radular tiny teeth gracing its hide. Instead, it gave a little whisper as it slid forward, and into her.

It tickled, then hurt, then felt unbearable until the agony somehow passed into an overwhelming ecstasy that moved through her whole body in perfusing, pleasure-pain waves. She squirmed as the rope shoved deeper and the baby waddled forward, as if spelunking toward her body while tethered to the cord.

The baby parted the slightly wrinkled lips of her vagina, like curtains into a theater whose stage he yearned to see. He slid forward, the cord he had kept coiled at his side now nesting within her body. The tumescent meat's throb where it sat among her organs felt somehow comforting, ticklish and intimate as it licked about and probed its way around. It caressed her insides, filled her with the warmth of a great and final violation. Death as orgasm, petit mort made grand guignol.

The baby pulled himself first within the snuggery of her thighs, then deeper into her belly. Then he lay there, motionless, at home in the stomach, crouched in the warm sheath of placenta quickening to yolky life around both him and the spiralling meat rope.

An ensouling sunshine glowed now from Claire's center, a heat that wouldn't have hurt even had it burnt at one-thousand degrees, Celsius.

She closed her eyes, whispered, "My butterfly," as her stomach swelled, first into a slight first trimester midden, then ballooned outward into a heaving globular gourd. Soon the baby would break free from the tender flesh chrysalis, and fly away on eyespot-patterned, parchment-thin, living velvet wings.

TONS-AWAY

Judith Pancoast

Three-hundred-pound Alicia punched that 800 number into her phone as fast as her acrylics could go.

After a week of hawk-eyeing the television for the Tons-Away infomercial, it was finally here, flashing *Miraculous Weight Loss in a Tiny Tablet! Call by midnight to get a second month's supply at 50% off!* in neon letters and filling her with hope. Her friend Kathy had been taking the stuff for three weeks and had already lost almost twenty pounds—and no matter what, Alicia was desperate to be next.

She'd noticed right away when Kathy started losing weight. Alicia had asked her how she was dropping the pounds.

"Oh, you know, just eating healthy. Reaching for an apple when I want a snack," Kathy had said.

Like hell. She and Kathy had been the fatty twins since elementary school, and together they'd tried every diet known to mankind. Kathy—who'd always claimed peanut butter cups were a legitimate source of protein—couldn't possibly have suddenly found some inner source of willpower that made it possible for her to "eat healthy." Perhaps it was something pharmaceutical.

Kathy had always been the larger of the two girls by about twenty pounds, which was why Alicia enjoyed hanging around her. Being in Kathy's company made her feel slimmer, and that was worth putting up with her boring stories about online dating, half of which were probably wishful thinking. Now Kathy was closing in and would soon weigh less than Alicia if she didn't figure out how she was doing it and get in on the deal, too.

While Kathy was in the bathroom, Alicia had gone through her nightstand drawer and found the bottle: Tons-Away. *Some best friend*, she thought. *Here we've been through every weight up and down together and she's not gonna share one that really works? What a joke.*

She'd never heard of this stuff and had no idea where to get it, but obviously, she couldn't ask Kathy without explaining why she'd been snooping. Instead, she googled *Where can I buy the Tons-Away tablet immediately* as soon as she could. Lots of results came up, but, weirdly, there didn't seem to be a website for the product. The only answers she could find all said to just watch for the infomercial.

The package was waiting on the porch the next day when she came home for lunch. Speedy! She hoped she lost weight that fast.

Excited about finally finding something she was confident would work, she went to the kitchen to take her first dose. She ignored the warnings and went straight to the directions: *Take one tablet daily with a full glass of water.* Getting the damned safety plastic off the bottle was frustrating as hell—and she almost lost one of her nails—but finally, a steak knife did the trick. She popped one of the giant pills in her mouth immediately. She hated drinking water, so she grabbed a 16-ounce bottle of Diet Coke from the fridge.

"What's that you just put in your mouth?"

Shit. She sees everything. Alicia hadn't even noticed her mother, Agnes, walk into the kitchen.

"Just a vitamin," she shot back.

"Since when do you take vitamins, Miss Health Queen of the Year?" Her mother's Long Island accent was the kind of nasal that cut through her brain like the constant buzz of a gnat.

Alicia heard the violent clinking of jars and bottles as she slammed the refrigerator shut. "Good one, Ma. I'm trying to turn over a new leaf. Today is the first day of the rest of your life and all that bullshit."

"Ha!" Agnes waddled out of the room.

She'd always been so supportive.

Alicia was shocked when she suddenly no longer felt like having lunch. The placebo effect, maybe? No pill she'd ever taken had worked *that* fast. For once, she wouldn't have to count calories or wonder whether the salad was really a better choice than the sub. Strangely elated, she tucked the bottle of pills in her purse, brought the packaging out to her car so her mother wouldn't see it, and went back to work.

That evening, Alicia went into her bedroom, took off her size 3X grey dress, and put on a giant Red Sox tee shirt and blue pull-on shorts. To prepare herself for the enormous change she was about to experience, she looked in the mirror—something she usually avoided at all costs.

There was Jabba the Hutt, wearing the colors of his favorite team, staring back at her. She was so sick of being fat, so sick of hearing "you'd be pretty if you lost weight," so sick of feeling gross. At twenty-five, she knew she was supposed to be in the prime of life, but she felt like an old lady, the mounds of fat too much for her five-foot frame.

Now, all of that was about to be behind her.

Suddenly, Alicia recalled the cherry pie she'd briefly spotted when she'd gotten the soda. Ma had gone to the bakery today and magnanimously left half for her.

"Oh, what the hell," she said to herself. "Might as well indulge one last time."

Every stair creaked as she made her way to the kitchen. No more worrying about the staircase collapsing—check that off the list of big girl concerns, along with the embarrassment of actually breaking a dining room chair, as she had one time when visiting a friend. Life was going to be easy as pie from now on. She chuckled.

Humming the tune to Neil Diamond's "Cherry Cherry," she cut a generous slice of pie and put it in the microwave, tapping her fingers on the old Formica countertop as she waited.

"I bought some French vanilla to go with that if ya want it."

Alicia jumped. "Ma! Why do you always sneak up on me like that?" She turned to see Agnes taking the ice cream carton out of the freezer.

"I just heard you warming up the pie, and thought you might like some ice cream, is all. I know French vanilla is your favorite with cherry pie." Ma smiled her weird false-teeth smile, which never, ever looked quite genuine.

"That was very thoughtful of you." Alicia settled herself at the kitchen table. She plopped a generous helping of golden ice cream onto the steaming wedge of pie. Plump cherries leaked out of the crust, staining the dessert plate red.

Agnes watched greedily as Alicia shoveled the first forkful into her mouth. As she chewed, ice cream and pie filling dribbled onto her chin. "This is delicious."

A red-hot pain seared through her stomach, so intense she clutched at her belly and fell to the floor, crying out.

"Alicia! What's wrong?"

The searing pain made it impossible to speak. Alicia could barely breathe.

"Should I call 9-1-1? What should I do?"

Alicia flopped onto her stomach, hoping the cold linoleum floor would ease her pain. She lay there, trying to focus on her breathing until the initial jolt subsided, and she was left with a throbbing burn. "I'm okay." She gasped. "I'm okay, Ma."

"Are you sure? You about gave me a heart attack!" Agnes wiped her hand across her perspiration-drenched brow. "What the hell happened?"

Alicia grabbed a kitchen chair and pulled herself up. "I don't know, but I don't think I'm gonna have any more pie right now. I'm just gonna go lie down."

Alicia found her usual spot on the couch, Ma plopped into the recliner, and they watched television for a while. When her mom called it a night, Alicia, feeling perfectly fine, went back into the kitchen and attempted another bite of the pie. She was on the floor again in minutes and knew her pie-eating days were over.

Once she'd recovered, she scraped the rest of her pie down the garbage disposal and went up to bed, only then wondering if the pill she'd taken had anything to do with the violent reaction to food. If she got sick every time she tried to eat something, she'd lose weight for sure, but the pain might not be worth it.

The next morning she was able to eat a banana and a half cup of plain yogurt without any troubles, even after swallowing her Tons Away pill first thing. Everything was fine until her call center lunch break.

She was sitting at an outdoor picnic table provided for the staff, waiting for one of the girls to come back with the haul from a fast-food run, when her stomach began to cramp. It was mild at first, and she thought maybe she just had to go, but her visit to the ladies' room didn't help matters. By the time the cheeseburger and fries were in front of her, the cramping had intensified, but not enough to keep her from biting into that juicy burger with its extra pickles and secret sauce. She was chasing the bite with a few fries when her stomach muscles abruptly seized. She involuntarily opened her mouth and vomited.

Her coworkers fled in disgust. Not one person offered to help as she once again clutched at her abdomen and moaned in pain. She sat there, alone, until the cramps subsided. Then she went in, grabbed her purse, said something about taking the rest of the day as sick time, and left.

On the way home her phone rang. It was Kathy.

"Hey Lish! Guess what? I hit a new milestone today. Thirty pounds lost! I'm back in my size 20 jeans!"

"That's great." Alicia tried to sound enthusiastic, but she was so jealous she could barely see straight. She couldn't help but suspect that Kathy had kept the "Tons-Away" a secret because *she* wanted to be the thinner one, and now, she was.

"I'm so happy for you. All that just by eating your fruits and veggies, huh?"

"That's right!" Kathy chirped. "You should try it. Carrot sticks are your friends."

Alicia's heart raced and a hot flash swept over her.

"Oh, just stop it. I know what you're doing, and it doesn't have anything to do with frigging Mr. McGregor's garden."

"What?" Kathy genuinely sounded confused.

"I found the Tons-Away in your nightstand."

The pause lasted so long that Alicia wondered if Kathy had hung up. She had time to pull into the driveway and turn off the car before a quiet voice came through the phone. It sounded as though Kathy were speaking through clenched teeth.

"You went through my nightstand drawer? Why would you do that?"

"Because I knew you had to be taking something. We've known about fruits and vegetables and frigging portion control all our lives and we've never been able to stick with it. You *had* to have help."

"So what if I did? That's no excuse to go through my private things."

"Why didn't you tell me? I thought we always helped each other with this stuff." Alicia was on the verge of tears.

"Oh, come on. You think I'm stupid? I know you've always felt superior to me because you're the thinner one. Now I finally had a real chance to become skinnier than you. Why would I share that?"

The inside of the car was starting to feel like a sauna; sweat was dripping from her forehead.

"I gotta go."

She struggled out of the car, peeling her fleshy thighs off the front seat, and toddled up the walkway.

Agnes was finishing the cherry pie when Alicia slogged through the back door.

"What are you doing home so early?" her mother asked.

"I don't feel good. I had another one of those attacks at work." She slid out of her flip-flops and collapsed into a reinforced kitchen chair.

"Maybe I should take you to the urgent care up the street." Agnes wiped cherry juice off her face with a paper towel. "We can go right now."

Alicia shook her head. "No, I don't want to right now. I'm just gonna go lie in my dark bedroom for a while."

"Okay then. Just holler if you need anything."

With the shades drawn and her rotary fan on high, Alicia rested on the soft chenille bedspread. Her muscles relaxed and she could breathe again. She began to wonder if she'd been too hard on Kathy.

I should call her back and say I'm sorry. Ask her if she's having any kind of a reaction to the Tons-Away.

Just as she was reaching for her cell phone, it chirped. It was Kathy.

Their voices collided through the airwaves as they apologized profusely to each other, promising never to deceive one another again, and renewing their lifelong friendship like lovers reunited after a tornado. Tears flowed and declarations of solidarity were made. Then Alicia had the courage to ask, "Have you had any kind of a reaction to the Tons-Away?"

"Like, what kind of reaction?"

"You know, like cramps or nausea. Anything like that?"

"No, not at all. In fact, it's just the opposite. I'm eating pretty much whatever I want, and I'm still losing weight. It's crazy. Why do you ask?"

"Oh, nothing. I only started taking it a couple of days ago, and I'm wondering about possible side effects, is all."

"Don't worry about it! Just enjoy your shrinking body. Next summer we're going to be the hottest babes on the beach!"

"That would be nice, wouldn't it? Well, I gotta go. It was so hot today, it really drained me. I think I'm gonna go to bed early."

"Okay then. Call me after you next weigh yourself, okay? I want us to share our good news from now on."

"I will. Goodnight."

She rolled over and smashed her face into the pillow. This was not good. If she *was* having a bad reaction to Tons-Away, and Kathy wasn't, that would be a disaster. Then she'd have to stop taking it, and Kathy, meanwhile, would become the next supermodel while she stayed obese and miserable. She *had* to make this work.

For the next week, she ate only bananas and plain yogurt. It worked like a charm. Exactly one week after taking the first pill, she stepped on the scale and was down an amazing eight pounds. She decided to celebrate, and picked up a loaded pizza on the way home from work.

The waiting room was packed when her mother brought her into the urgent care facility, but Alicia was moaning so loudly that the triage nurse got her into a curtained room right away. The first bite of pizza had sent her stomach into spasms so painful that she puked and kept gagging even after there was nothing left to upchuck, and she'd dry-heaved all the way to the clinic. When the nurse asked her if she'd been on any medications, she conveniently forgot about the Tons-Away tablets. No use bringing that up.

"What about those new vitamins you've been taking, huh?" her mother chimed. "God knows what's in those."

The nurse had looked at her expectantly and Alicia sighed. "They're just plain old One-a-Day vitamins from the pharmacy. My mother likes to make a big deal out of everything."

After the nurse left, Ma paced the small room, clutching her handbag. "It could be an ulcer, or maybe you have a gallstone. I had a gallstone once. Just one big one. Most people have a bunch of little rocks but I only—"

A dark, handsome, young doctor walked into the room. He extended a hand to Alicia. "Hello, I'm Dr. Bhattacharjee. So, you're having some stomach issues, eh?"

"That's putting it mildly, doctor," Agnes said. "I just don't know what to do. I'm so worried."

Dr. Bhattacharjee nodded. "I see, madam." He turned to Alicia again. "Can you tell me what's been going on?"

Minutes later, Alicia was wheeled into the procedure room for an endoscopy. Thankfully, her mother had been told to wait, and Alicia imagined her sitting in the waiting room in one of those hard, plastic chairs, chewing gum like a madwoman and thumbing through an old, tattered copy of *AARP*. The thought made her chuckle a bit.

They'd given her a Valium and she was floating along, not a care in the world. Now she opened wide as the physician's assistant sprayed the back of her throat with a numbing concoction so she wouldn't gag when the scope went down.

She was having a waking dream about cherry pie, not hearing the on-call gastroenterologist as she said, "We're just going to put this camera down your throat and take a look at what's going on down there. Open wide. Here we go, you're doing great, we're almost...there. *Oh!*"

The doctor jumped back from the table.

"Holy shit! What the hell is that?" said a male voice.

"What? What are you talking about? What's wrong?" Alicia wasn't sure if she was saying the words out loud.

Something wriggled on the monitor. A very big something, too big to be in her body. It was coming closer to the camera. It looked like a knob with hair-like hooks.

"Christ! I think it's a tapeworm. A... very... large... tapeworm!" someone said.

"A *what?*" Suddenly Alicia was wide awake. "A tapeworm? A fucking *tapeworm?*"

She began to gag uncontrollably, which was very difficult with a long wire snaking down her throat.

Two nurses rushed forward and held her down. "Be still," one of them said, "We've got this under control." But they didn't. They truly didn't.

One of the technicians began to pull the camera out. The wire burned her throat as it came up, and now she could feel something large rising behind, like she was about to throw up a Nerf ball. The camera came out and then a soft...*thing*...glided past her epiglottis, sliding along her soft palate and making her gag and gag and gag. Her eyeballs felt like they were about to pop out of their sockets, her head was about to explode. She felt wetness as her bladder let go, drenching the johnny gown and sheet beneath her. Her body suddenly sat bolt upright of its own accord, as though she'd been jolted with electricity.

Her mouth opened so wide it felt like her jaw was about to crack as the worm's head pushed its way through and rode out on a trail of green slime, its numerous suckers opening and closing. As the neck slowly appeared from her maw, the head flopped down on her chest and allowed itself to be pushed by the ever elongating, segmented body.

"We need to get her into surgery, *stat!*"

Alicia couldn't breathe. The thing was blocking her airway so that even a breath through her nose was impossible. Meanwhile, the worm segments kept on coming, until, halfway down the hall to the operating room, a geyser of blood gushed out along with the last part of the tail, which was entwined around a substantial piece of Alicia's intestines. She took one agonized breath, and her heart stopped.

Life-saving measures were undertaken to no avail. She was pronounced dead at 7:59 pm. She weighed just shy of three hundred pounds.

No one ever heard the message left on her cell phone during the whole ordeal. It was someone from the Tons-Away company, calling to inform her that they'd mixed up her order with that of a six-foot-seven, 588-pound man. She'd gotten the extra-large dose meant for him. They were very sorry for the mix-up, and if she could simply return the remaining tablets they'd be glad to refund her money and send her another shipment of the correct dosage, absolutely free.

Of course, she'd just have to pay for the shipping.

TRIBUTES

William Curnow

Downes saw it on the Regent's Canal, on the stretch approaching Limehouse Basin. He was taking photographs for an evening course, trying to capture the reflections of buildings in the water. There was no wind to hamper him; he'd had a good afternoon.

The first he knew of it was a shadow passing over the water. Looking up, he saw something overhead: dark, dripping. He had the impression of a sodden bin bag inflated by the wind, but it was gone behind the buildings before he could work out what he was seeing.

Uneasy, puzzled, Downes resumed his position on the towpath, squatting down to get closer to the water, trying to line up a converted warehouse just so. The first picture was blurred, the second a little better. He adjusted for the light and took another.

He was about ready to move on when it came again. Very low this time, swooping down over the water, spreading itself out as it followed the course of the canal. There was an awful smell as it swept past, rotting carpets and bad meat. Instinctively, he shied away. Perhaps that saved him.

It moved quickly, too quickly for something of its bulk, and then it was fifty yards away, getting lower all the time. Finally, he saw what it was heading for. A swan, slow to react. Just beginning to turn as it was engulfed. The bird struggled, wings beating, the surface of the water black, rippling like polythene.

A moment later, Downes started at a cyclist's bell on the path behind him. He wanted to stop the rider, say, 'Look, do you see what's just happened?' but the commotion had subsided, and the surface of the canal was clear again, no swan to be seen. No black thing. Nothing. Dazed, he stood aside to let the bike pass.

Victoria Park. Downes sat on a bench, cycling through the pictures. Breathing too quickly, heart skittering. Only when the screen turned black did he realise that he'd captured it. Not much, a blur, badly framed so you wouldn't be able to tell which way was up if you didn't know already. Enough for him, though.

Downes pushed on. A second picture, further away now. The swan already in shot. At that size, he couldn't make out any details. He had to wait until he got home to see anything more, the computer seeming to take forever to boot up, but at last he transferred the pictures. *Do you want to keep the originals on the camera?* the computer asked him.

A slideshow. Hurrying through the pictures he'd gone there to take. The basin, the locks, a Polish beer bottle on a bench. And there it was. He paused the slideshow, marvelled over the instinct that had made him take the picture.

Even on the bigger screen, there wasn't much he could make sense of in that first picture. The more he looked, the less he saw. A dark surface, a little rough, torn in places, stretched like shrink-wrap in others.

The second made things no clearer. He got more of a sense of the size of the thing, but though he could now see parts of the buildings and a stretch of canal, there was no clear definition to the edges. The more he stared, the more the question of where it started and ended became meaningless. Everything contained it, or nothing contained it, depending on how he chose to look.

Downes enlarged both pictures until they started to lose detail, then he played around with them. Enhancing this bit, sharpening that. Hours with Photoshop, surrounded by prints, none of which told him what he wanted to know. Whatever had happened at the canal remained a mystery.

Downes slept badly, woke screaming, fighting the duvet. Even when he understood that it was just a dream, he couldn't get back to sleep until he'd searched the whole of the flat. Sweat turned clammy on his back as he paced from room to room. All was as it should be. The only sound a car in the street outside. Nevertheless, he didn't sleep much that night.

His tutor, an earnest, eager woman, keen to find some aspect to praise, however small, reviewed everyone's work at the start of the class.

'Good,' she said when she came to him. 'This is interesting.'

He didn't see immediately what she was looking at, but he didn't need to. How it had gotten into his portfolio he didn't know, but there it was: the indefinable black print he knew so well now.

'What is it?'

'I don't know exactly,' he said.

It wasn't a lie, but it was hardly the whole story either, and he worried that she was going to ask him further questions, but instead she called over the rest of the group and talked to them about the qualities of accident and spontaneity, before moving on.

Back at the canal. A week later. He'd tried to forget, couldn't get it out of his head. It troubled him, the descending dark. The floor littered with prints.

A bearded man with a camera and tripod occupied the spot where he had taken the picture. Downes nodded to him as he walked past. The man was still there four hours later as he made his way back to the station. The next day, too, when he returned.

Downes wanted to ask if he seen it, too. But he dreaded the answer either way. Was this what madness felt like?

Instead, he took photographs of everything, spending hours each evening searching for some clue in them. There were times when he thought he had something, but each new lead was only another disappointment. Tendrils revealed themselves as weed; he lost count of the number of tarpaulins that fooled him.

He lingered over a speck in the corner of one particular picture. Enlarged it. Could that be what he was looking for? Sometimes he thought it was, but by the time he got it to a size where he could see it properly, it lacked all definition. Even if he'd found it, he was none the wiser.

Downes began to doubt himself. He tried to rationalise it. 'A great big wet bin bag of death!' he said to himself, and laughed, though the laughter wasn't quite as convincing as he'd have liked, and he couldn't shake off the feeling that something bad was going to happen. It came back to him in the middle of the night like a sudden cramp. He woke, crying.

On his next visit, the bearded photographer was gone. Now that it was too late, Downes regretted not asking the question.

He sat on a bench for hours, staring at the reflections of the buildings in the water. He almost wanted it to come back, so that he could prove it to himself. He set the camera to take pictures at ten second intervals, put in a new memory card and pointed it towards the canal.

At last, with the light beginning to go, Downes packed up. It was then that he smelled it. The same stench as before. Only there for a moment, but that was long enough. He looked round, struggling with the camera bag, trying to get himself ready for what was coming. But it was nowhere. He ran a few paces in one direction, then the other, trying to pick up the smell. Nothing.

Then he saw the bearded man. He was coming along the path towards Downes. Did he feel relief or annoyance? Perhaps it would not come now that there were two of them.

The bearded man was upon Downes before he knew it.

'You're waiting for it, too.'

His breath smelled bad as he leaned in, too close. Downes felt sudden anger at the man's presumption.

Up close, the man was a wreck. Unkempt beard, red eyes, grey-skinned as though he hadn't had a proper night's sleep in a long time. Not as old, though, as Downes had first taken him for.

His name was Johnson, he said. Martin Johnson. Not like the rugby player. Laughed. He was twitchy. There was a smell about him. Masked by the reek of unwashed flesh, clothes. Something damp, mouldering.

'What are you talking about?' Downes asked, guarded.

Johnson dismissed Downes' question, as if it were of no consequence.

'I can tell you about it.' A sly smile. 'If you like. You want to know more, don't you?'

Downes gave up pretending. Needed to know.

'And if I do, you're the man to ask?'

He nodded. Shuffled from one foot to the other in an agitated fashion.

'Maybe, maybe.'

'So, what is it?'

Johnson looked round nervously. Licked dry, cracked lips.

'Not here.'
'Where then?'
'I'm thirsty.'
In the pub. A broken-down old boozer. Hard looks from the locals. Two pints of beer and a packet of crisps for Johnson. At Downes' expense.

He watched with distaste as Johnson ran a finger down the packet, taking great relish in licking the flavourings off his fingertip.

'Tell me about it.'
'What do you want to know?'
'Tell me what it is.'
Johnson shrugged.
'I don't know that.'
'Where it comes from, then.'
'Somewhere in the dark tidal reaches? How should I know? Do I look like David fucking Attenborough?'
'So, what do you know?'
A long pause.
'I know what it wants.' Followed by the smack of his lips.
'And what does it want?'
But Johnson wasn't listening. Instead, HE WAS looking over Downes' shoulder, out the window. He became fidgety after that. Refused to say any more, announced he needed a piss and headed for the back of the pub. The minutes passed slowly. Only gradually did Downes realise he wasn't coming back.

Downes asked the barman about the man when he came round collecting empties.

'Friend of yours, is he?'
'Not exactly. Is he a regular?'
The barman laughed.
'Not if Viv catches him in here.'
Downes stayed for another pint in case Johnson returned. Didn't. The atmosphere thawed.

He nodded to the barman as he left. The man shook his head in pity.

Downes got the notion into his head on the journey home. *I know what it wants.* He kept looking over his shoulder, waited until the Northern Line platform was empty, then doubled back on himself. Took the Victoria Line instead. Couldn't help scanning the faces at each stop, even so.

Downes slipped the key into the lock, trying to make as little noise as possible. He tiptoed through the flat, checking each room in turn. Finding nothing. His relief tempered by the sense that something had been deferred again.

He didn't sleep that night. Sat in front of the computer, glass of whisky in one hand. *I know what it wants.*

Downes found Johnson again soon enough. Scouring the pubs along the canal the next afternoon. Different pub, just gone opening time, Johnson looking as though he'd been there for hours already.

'What kept you?' he said.

'It wasn't easy finding the only pub round here that you're not barred from.'

Johnson bared rotten teeth in a semblance of a smile, raised his glass.

Downes got himself a pint and a double whisky. He downed the whisky while waiting for his change.

'Tell me what you have to say. No tricks this time,' Downes told Johnson, not wanting to prolong the encounter.

Johnson's mood had changed completely; now he wanted to talk, regale Downes his theories.

'It's like all the banality of the city coalesced into one. All the psychogeographers, all the City Boys and Brexiteers. All those administrators and cleaners, they walked it into mud and stone. Into concrete and bitumen. We all wanted it to happen. We're gagging for it.'

He took a sip from his pint, then wiped his lips. A smear of blood left on the back of his hand.

'It's getting stronger all the time. The first time I saw it, it was no bigger than a fox. It fed on rats. Now it eats dogs, geese. Swans.'

He let the last hang in the air, and Downes wondered whether his encounter had been observed, after all.

'All in the space of three months. What do you imagine its natural progression would be? Children? How long would their little fat arms satisfy it do you think? Days? Weeks?'

He was enjoying having someone to listen to him.

'Yesterday, you said you knew what it wants.'

'Did I?' His smile was malicious. 'I'm not well, you know.' He banged the side of his head with the glass. Downes winced. 'Things go missing up here.'

People were looking in their direction. Muttering.

'How many times have you seen it?'

'A dozen, perhaps. Maybe less, maybe more. I watched it grow.' He sounded proud of that fact.

'Could you have stopped it?' Downes asked.

'Perhaps.' He shrugged. 'Too late now.'

'So, what happens now?'

'Now?' He snickered. 'Now we let things take their course.'

'That doesn't bother you?'

Johnson got up abruptly. 'You want to know what it wants, come with me.'

He was swaying, couldn't stand properly, beckoning for Downes to follow.

'Or are you all mouth?' he shouted.

Downes finished off his pint. He didn't want Johnson to see that he was rattled. Downes didn't look at the other drinkers on the way out. What was on their faces? Pity? Contempt? It didn't matter. He had to know.

As Johnson led them into unfamiliar back streets, Downes hung back, wondering how dangerous the man was; Johnson glanced back, beckoning whenever Downes got too far behind for his liking.

'Where are we going?' Downes called to him several times.

'You'll see,' was all he would say.

At last, Johnson came to a halt. An empty street. The backs of houses, windows broken. Derelict. At the far end, a back yard, the wooden door rotted in places. Something growing in the frame. Downes gagged at the stink as he ducked beneath it, careful not to touch anything.

If Downes had thought the smell was bad outside, it was nothing compared to now. There were bin bags everywhere he looked, their contents spewed on to the ground. A dank, rotting mush underfoot.

'Here we are!' Johnson said triumphantly. 'Home again.'

The house was worse than the yard. The kitchen floor filled with washing up tubs, more on the worktops. There had perhaps been something in the grey water once, nothing now.

'What is this?' Downes said, kicking the nearest tub. Its contents went everywhere. Greasy water sloshed over broken tiles.

'Don't do that!' Johnson shouted.

'What is this?' Downes shouted at him, appalled.

'Why, do you like it?'

He was tired, wanted answers. Johnson had none.

Downes kicked over another bucket and Johnson came at him. No strength to it, though.

Downes pushed him away. Johnson tripped. Went down heavily. Hit his head. Didn't get up again.

For a moment, Downes thought he was dead, but then he was sitting up, laughing.

'You're for it now.'

He spat out a tooth.

'I'm leaving,' Downes said.

Johnson shook his head, whether to clear it, or to reject Downes' words, Downes didn't know, didn't care.

'You'll be back,' he shouted after Downes, bubbles of blood and snot forming from his nostrils, but he didn't follow.

He lasted a week. A week of imagining it draped over him every time he closed his eyes. Each night, the dream was worse, more suffocating than the last.

Soon, there was no escape when he was awake either. It was with him everywhere he went. Something black and snaky on the edge of vision. A fist of membrane.

Johnson was right. He knew Downes would find him again. Would have to find him.

Downes returned to the house. The tubs were gone, but Johnson was still there. He started shouting when he saw Downes, retreated upstairs, cursed at him from between rotting bannisters.

'I'm sorry about last time,' Downes said. 'I lost my temper. It won't happen again. Please, I need to know.'

'Well, you're out of luck then, aren't you?'

Downes put a foot on the bottom stair.

'Don't come up here,' Johnson warned.

He threw something. It clattered against the wall above Downes' head. Downes retreated into the front hall.

'What do you want?' he called. 'What will make it right?'

He thought Johnson hadn't heard, was about to repeat the question, then he heard Johnson whisper.

'A tribute.'

'What?'

'You'll have to pay.'

Johnson took Downes to the local corner shop, selected things from the shelves at random. Washing powder, gram flour, candles, tissues, oil. Cheap lager.

'This one's for me,' he said, opening it there and then.

Johnson didn't offer to carry any of it.

'Leave them there,' Johnson commanded when they were back in the kitchen.

'Are we done?' Downes asked. 'Are we even?'

'We're even.'

'You can show me?'

'I can show you.'

'Now?'

Johnson shook his head.

'I'm a busy man. Things to do.'

'When then?'

'Tomorrow.'

He got Downes to meet him in another pub, somewhere in the industrial estates south of the river. Not banned from this one. Not yet. But he had was drunk, so give it time.

Downes wanted to get going, get it over with, but Johnson wouldn't be moved. Downes had to buy him a pint of lager, a coke for himself. Johnson looked in even worse shape than the day before. His face covered in sores, lank hair falling out.

When he opened his mouth, Downes saw several teeth had crumbled away. The smell was terrible.

'How far is it?' he asked.

'Not far. Be patient.'

Johnson took an age to drink the pint, but finally was ready.

'Come on then,' he said, as if Downes had been holding them up.

Outside, it was a cold night, but Downes was grateful for that. The smell was muted. Johnson seemed uncertain where to go, peered around him, then made a decision. Downes wondered whether this was going to be another wild goose chase.

Johnson crossed the road without looking. A sustained horn, bleeding into the squeal of rubber on asphalt, and a white van came to a halt. Johnson bounced off the bonnet. The driver started to get out, swearing at him.

Downes could have walked away; he intervened.

'Sorry,' he shouted as he ran across the road. 'He's not well.' Hardly a lie.

'I could have hit him.' The driver shouted at Johnson: 'I could have hit you, mate.' He was shaking with anger and shock. Then he saw Johnson up close and stopped.

'Fucking hell,' he said, looking at Downes with revulsion. 'What's wrong with him?'

He retreated to the van as Downes led Johnson away.

'He shouldn't be on the streets,' he shouted as they reached the pavement. The van pulled away, door slamming shut even as it moved. Downes saw the man's face caught for a second, then light reflected off the windscreen and he was gone.

Johnson acted like it was nothing, lurched off, led him into the industrial estate. Parked-up lorries. Shuttered warehouses behind high fences. Rusting skips full of dirty water, incubating who knew what. No one else on the street. The yards here a poor state of repair. Many empty. Importer/exporters, couriers, a forbidding silo with 'Party Food Caterers' on the side.

Downes lost his sense of direction as Johnson meandered, doubling back on himself. He thought he could hear the river ahead, but the next moment it was behind them. The traffic sounds grew muted. He took out his phone but couldn't get a fix on their location.

If he went back now, he'd never find it. Never get the answer. Johnson only a few months left in him at this rate.

A dead fox under a car's wheel arch, surrounded by its own vomit. Other signs, too. The bodies of birds, eaten out from inside. Something covered in fur. Liquefied. Unidentifiable. Downes knew they were getting close.

The building was on the river. A nineteenth century warehouse, Downes guessed. Derelict now. Trees grew from what remained of the roof. The windows empty.

The sign on the fence said: 'Unsafe structure.' Underneath: 'Warning: Guard dogs patrol these premises.'

Johnson had a torch. He'd sobered up, pacing around as he waited for Downes to catch up.

'Is it safe?' Downes asked.

Johnson gestured to the sign.

'Don't worry. No dogs here. They won't stay – they turn on their handlers.'

At the rear, the wall had fallen away. Someone had made a crude attempt to cover it with corrugated iron. Johnson tore at it with bloodied hands, created a gap wide enough for a man, crawled through.

Downes followed. On the other side, weeds grew to waist high. Johnson out of breath, but triumphant.

'Here we are then.'

He led Downes up a fire escape. Metal complained with every step. The padlock had vanished from the door at the top, a chain hanging loose.

'Are you coming?' Johnson complained.

Downes looked out over the river, fast flowing tonight, readied himself, and followed.

It was warm inside. The damp warmth of a hothouse. Johnson was already sweating, oily beads running down his forehead. The room had been an office, perhaps. There were signs that someone has been sleeping here. Empty tins, a filthy blanket, notepads. The shopping bags Downes had bought from the corner shop, contents scattered. A tribute, Johnson had said.

Johnson's camera was set up by the window, focussed on the floor of the warehouse. Downes checked it, but it was too dark to make anything out through the viewfinder. He pressed the shutter release. The flash went off and he got a glimpse of something below. The floor glistened, wet, oily. Chemical.

'What are you doing?' Johnson shouted at him.

From below, there was a wet sound like the tide slapping against a harbour. The stench was appalling, caustic. Downes couldn't breathe, coughed and spluttered. Black mucus dripped from his nose. He wiped it away with the back of his hand, but more came.

As Johnson fumbled with the torch, the beam skittered across the warehouse floor. Downes tried to concentrate, ignore the smell. What was he seeing? He grabbed Johnson's wrist, steadying the light. Then he saw the dogs. Or what was left of them.

They don't stay, Johnson had said, but that wasn't true. They stayed, all right. They never left.

The handlers, too? Disgusted, Downes pushed him away. He didn't need the light to see the whole floor was moving. How had it got so large?

'Christ,' he said, appalled, 'what have you done?'

'You wanted to see this,' Johnson said gleefully. 'Think of it as a taste of what's to come.'

'What have you done?'

But of course, Downes knew.

Was this Johnson's idea of a trap? Maybe he thought he could do a deal with it; thought he had done a deal with it.

Whatever his plan, Downes didn't give him a chance. The chain he'd taken from the door caught Johnson on the side of the jaw. His head flicked back, and the torch flew from his hand as Downes brought it round for another blow.

There was only one way this could end. Johnson hit the rail, overbalanced, fell.

Downes heard him hit. But that wasn't the worst thing.

'My leg,' Johnson shouted, slurring, made stupid from the fall. 'You've broken my bloody leg.'

The torch followed him over. As it lit up his face, Downes saw understanding dawn.

'It'll have you too,' Johnson shouted before a torn edge, soft as marshmallow, swept over him.

Downes stayed to watch. It took hours.

In the following days, he brought other tributes.

118

BURN

Wayne Kyle Spitzer

Because the windows were bulletproof, it all had to come out through the main entrance, and that included the grand piano in the Entrance Hall—which we wheeled recklessly against the doorframe before upending it with a huff and shoving it down the stairs, where it sounded briefly, chaotically, as it impacted each step. By then I was leaning on one side of the door while Fiona leaned on the other, looking on: at our friends as they started busting up the instrument below with bats and feet and sledgehammers, but also at the overgrown North Lawn of the White House and its spitting, crackling bonfire; at the tricked out Hondas and Toyotas as they continued pouring onto the field and bringing more—more beer kegs and more gasoline, more children of the Flashback, more us.

"Look at it, big sister," I said, finding her already staring at me in the flickering semi-dark, "It's like poetry, I swear."

"Green Room," she answered calmly, seeming almost to smolder. "And stop calling me that."

My eyes flicked up and down her body—something they'd been doing a lot of lately—but I don't think she noticed. Of course she was right; a lot had changed since our first burn—not the least of which was my voice—and calling her that no longer seemed appropriate. She, too, had changed—becoming less like a big sister (or even a mother) and more like an equal, even if, at 19, she still had a good 4 years on me.

"Okay, babe," I said, winking at her. I kicked the pedestal and candelabra next to me over with a resounding crash. "So let's do it."

And we went to work, Fiona pulling down the pictures and the red and green curtains while I took my bat to the china cabinet—smashing the glass as though it were a thin layer of ice, sending shards of it flying, bludgeoning the green plates and gold leafed vases like piñatas, like the shattered skulls of imagined enemies, until 243 years of history lay a glistening wreck at my feet—just so much broken detritus to be burned with the rest; just so much dust and memory to be erased and finally forgotten. At which I looked at Fiona and she looked back, smiling, her teeth large and slightly crooked, carnivorous—because it was a pleasure to burn, an ecstasy to burn.

By the time we rejoined the party, the bonfire was licking at the boughs of the maple trees and the staging had been erected for Calvin's speech—staging he was already ascending, gripping the rungs with one hand while holding a rolled up document—or documents—in the other, the firelight reflecting off his glasses.

"So what's he going to talk about?" I asked Fiona, heaving one of the two chairs I'd brought onto the fire—its red upholstery going up like dry paper, creating plumes of black smoke.

"How should I know? He's barely said two words to me since North Carolina." She pitched the framed pictures she was carrying—one of a dude she'd called Jimmy Carter—onto the roaring heap. "Look, Leif. I know he's something of a hero to you ... but you don't know him like I do. And I'm telling you, his heart's no longer in this. The Burning. It hasn't been since Georgia. At least."

I threw the other chair onto the pyre. "But it was his idea in the first place—wasn't it? Isn't that what you said—"

"I've said a lot of things," she snapped, and used her whole body to throw the second picture. "People change, Leif. At least some do. Others just get old."

I paused, thinking about that. Had something happened between them, like a fight? What did that mean, 'Others just get old?'"

"Okay, wild children, listen up!" cried Calvin from the top of the platform—and waved the rolled up documents to get everyone's attention. "Hear, hear! You're having *way* too much fun."

It took a minute but eventually the car stereos and loose chatter diminished and the silence reasserted itself—or nearly so, for the fire continued to crack and to pop and to roar like a veritable furnace.

"But then, why else would God have invented adolescence—if not to have fun?"

Hoots and cheers, whistles and applause.

"And that we have had. From Austin to Baton Rouge and Jackson to Montgomery, from Atlanta to Raleigh and Norfolk to Richmond ... to come at last to Washington, and the seat of Old Power itself. To come at last to the very pinnacle of what we set out to do—which was to loot and burn every vestige of what had come before; every deed and every banknote, every binding contract and article of law, and to cede them back to whatever chaos must ultimately rule our lives."

He looked out over us, his friends, his people, and seemed to reflect. "And yet I wonder—what remains of the old world and the old laws to douse and burn? I mean, besides these ..." He lifted the rolled papers above his head, inciting raucous applause. "These relics of a bygone age— which Leif and Fiona have so brazenly liberated? Well, I tell you, there is one thing— but we'll save that for later, when they return ..."

I looked at Fiona and she looked back. Were we going back to the Archives?

"For now, let us commend these, one U.S. Constitution and one Declaration of Independence, to the fires of a New World— a world as young and savage and beautiful as we are, for it has yet to see even its 30th month, just as we have yet to see our 30th year. And afterward, afterward, I'll have a special announcement. Right now it's time to party; and to dance on the grave of that which is old and dead—and which never served us anyway. *Salud!*"

"*Salud!*" echoed the crowd, raising their plastic cups.

And then he was unfurling the documents and dropping them into the fire, which hissed and popped and seemed almost alive, and Fiona and I were shoving our way through the crowd— both of us, I think, wondering where we were being sent, and more importantly, what this 'special announcement' might be.

"Babe," said Calvin, descending the ladder, and I looked away as he and Fiona embraced (briefly), I'm not sure why.

"Got another job for you two—if you're up to it."

"If we're up to it," said Fiona, and laughed, at which there was an awkward silence I didn't understand. "I know: You want us to take a group of bad apples and put down the Norsemen. Am I right?"

The Norsemen were the older group who's territory we'd violated in order to access the White House and National Mall— and who were bound to cause us trouble if we didn't leave soon.

"Wrong. I want you to go to the National Museum and liberate the Star-Spangled Banner—the flag, not the song—and bring it here to be burned."

Fiona shot me a glance. "He's a vandal, Leif, not a fighter."

"I'm not a killer, if that's what you mean," he retorted, then turned away and watched the fire, hands on his hips. "Nor will I let any of us be. I mean, if I've said it once I'll say it again: this isn't about bloodshed. It's not even about rebellion. It's more about ..." He paused—as though saying anything else could only lead to regret.

"I thought it was about nothing," said Fiona, softly. "That that was its beauty—it was wildness for the sake of wildness. Passion for the sake of passion. Isn't that what you said?" She laughed with surprising bitterness. "Different context, I guess."

"It was about filling the nothing," he said, still facing away. "And letting go. Until ... But then—you haven't had to think about any of that ... have you? No one's made you king."

"And cue the Messiah Complex," fumed Fiona, which I took as my cue to leave; to give them space—to let them hash it out, whatever it was—after which I wandered over to one of the kegs and filled a cup, reckoning that next to a roaring fire wasn't the best place to keep beer—because it tasted like piss, literally. Nor did I stop at one but downed three in rapid succession, wondering what Calvin had meant by 'filling the nothing' and 'letting go,' and about being king—not to mention starting a sentence with 'until' ... but never finishing it.

And I guess I must have stood there for a while, because I distinctly recall watching the same group of teens—their arms laden with destruction—moving back and forth between the fire and the White House—the fucking White House!—to the point that I began feeling shitty about what we'd done; and even a little sick to my stomach. But then Fiona returned jingling Calvin's keys and we were firing up his Mustang convertible, and the next thing I remember she was piloting us down 14th Street NW past buildings with Doric columns (now choked in prehistoric ivy) and a pair of grazing stegosaurs and at least one giant millipede; all the way to Constitution Avenue and the National Museum; which I took special note of only because I was trying not to look at her body—something she noticed, I'm sure, but didn't seem to mind—because she just glanced at me beneath the blood red sky and smiled—toothily. Carnivorously.

It was the sort of thing you had to actually *see;* up close, personal—as up close and personal as the glass would allow, anyway—to fully appreciate; to fully understand that this was *it,* the flag that inspired the national anthem, the actual Fort McHenry garrison flag, a thing more than 40 feet high and maybe 30 feet long, laying at an angle in a climate-controlled black room, or a room that *had* been climate-controlled, until the Flashback, until the lights had gone out from Anchorage to Miami.

"Oh, say can you see," I sang, moving my flashlight over the material, which was tattered and torn, "By the dawn's early light ..."

I grinned and trailed off, letting the silence take control, letting the room buzz, and we just stood there.

"What so proudly we hailed," sang Fiona at length, her voice cracking a little, "at the twilight's last gleaming." She took a breath in the dark. "Whose broad stripes and bright stars ... through the perilous fight ... O'er the ramparts we watched— were so gallantly streaming ..."

Then, together: "And the rocket's red glare, the bombs bursting in air, gave proof through the night ... that our flag was still there." We both took a breath. "Oh, say does that star-spangled *ba-anner* yet wave ... o'er the *land* of the free ... and the *home* ... of the ... brave."

And again there was a silence, as perfect and deep as anything I'd ever experienced, either then or since.

"Fuck," I said.

"Yeah," said Fiona. "Fuck."

I looked at the sparse starfield illuminated in her beam.

"They're all gone," I said, and lowered my flashlight. "Everyone who ever touched this. Those who first sowed it;

those who stood in its shadow. Those who built this building to preserve it—all gone."

"Yeah," whispered Fiona. "It's just us."

"I don't know, big sis—I mean 'babe.' But do you ever wonder if—like, we're doing the right thing?"

"No."

"Okay. Well. Why is that, exactly?"

"Because there is no right thing. I mean, maybe there was ... before the universe just—went bugfuck. Before everyone just vanished. But now? What's right and what's wrong, Leif? I mean, what could possibly make any difference—one way or the other?"

"I don't know. It just seems that, like—"

"You're sounding like Calvin; don't go there. Because, I'm telling you, he's not who you think he is. Not anymore. He's—"

"Evolving?"

"Aging. Just aging. There's a difference."

"It's going to happen," I said. "We can't stay teenagers for—"

"Can't we?" She shook her head. "Maybe you don't see yourself ... but I do. See you, that is. And let me tell you—*you're a fire.*" She touched my hand where it gripped the sledgehammer. "And fires need to keep moving, keep consuming," She raised my arm gently, assuredly, until I dropped my flashlight completely and took the hammer in both hands. "... or they burn out."

And then I swung, harder than I ever had before, harder even than when I'd destroyed the china hutch, punching a white crater into the glass as big my head, causing cracks to spread out in rings, like a contagion, I thought, or a cancer, until I swung again and the head of the hammer smashed clean through, enough so that I had to fight to pull it back out, after which Fiona joined in and we smashed through the glass together, not all at once but blow after blow, until the bitter shards lay all around us and we fell to the flag's faded cloth, kissing and groping each other with abandon, unfastening and working off each other's clothes, fucking like it was the end of the world, which of course it was—consuming each other like paper in fire.

It goes without saying that I was driving too fast; I was 15 and had just gotten laid. Add to that my inexperience—and a spike strip laid across the road—and, well, you probably have some idea how we ended up in the fountain of the Ronald Reagan Building with Old Glory folded up and sticking out of the trunk. All I know for certain is that we were both injured, Fiona seriously—to the extent that the blood from her head had fouled her left eye and she couldn't stop shaking; which is how I noticed the figures approaching us from behind (I saw them in the rearview mirror when I removed Calvin's doo-rag, to stop her bleeding).

"Fiona, listen—we—we gotta get out of here. Can you walk?"

"What is it?" she asked, weakly, deliriously, looking around like a blind person (which I suppose she was), bleeding profusely.

I squinted at the figures—there were more of them now—saw long beards and jackboots; rifles, riot gear, motorcycle helmets to which horns had been attached.

"Norsemen," I said. "Lots of them. Hold on."

I threw open my door and went around, noticing how exposed we were, how exposed the entrance to the building was.

"I'm going to put you across my back, okay? Just hang on."

"Okay."

"Here we go—"

And then I heaved her across my back and we went, hustling up 14th Street NW even as the Norsemen opened fire and the pavement sparked all around us—all the way to something called the M.I.M. Museum, the door of which I kicked in awkwardly before carrying Fiona up a flight of steps and laying her before a giant mural, after which I collapsed against the nearby wall—the window of which promptly exploded.

"Fuck!" I cursed, lying flat on my stomach, then crawled through the glass to Fiona where I shielded her lithe body with my own.

"It's okay, we're okay," I said quickly, even as she started to hyperventilate. "We're fine. They don't know we're not armed—they don't know we're not armed. They're not going to come in. Not yet."

I wrapped her in my arms and held her tight, even as the other windows were blown out and glass rained down. And then, just as suddenly as it had begun, it was over; at least for the moment—after which I lifted my head, slowly, cautiously, and listened.

Nothing. A squawk of a pterodactyl, maybe, way off in the distance.

"Leif?" managed Fiona, groggily. "Are you there?"

I squeezed her tightly, stunned that she couldn't feel it. *"Shh-shhh,"* I said, stroking her hair, which was matted with blood, kissing her forehead.

At last a voice called, "We just want the girl. Give us the girl; vacate the House and the Mall, and we're done here. All right?"

I held Fiona close trying to still her trembling—realizing, in the process, that I was trembling myself. *"Shhh—*it's okay," I said, finding her hand, enveloping it in my own. "Everything is going to be okay."

"Aww, you're sweet," she said, her voice faint, papery. "But it's not. It never has been. You know that. Even before the Flashback."

"Shhh," I repeated, and diverted my eyes to the mural, which depicted, in stark black and white, seemingly all the atrocities human beings had ever committed—most of which I was unfamiliar with, the Holocaust and Hiroshima being obvious exceptions.

"They're right, you know," she said, softly, having followed my gaze. "The lights in the clouds. The shapes ... in that beautiful borealis, that came with the Flashback. They're right about us."

But I only stared at the painting, at the depictions of medieval torture and Mayan beheadings, at the lifeless, flattened cities and mounds of emaciated corpses, like driftwood; at the piles of skulls and perfect, white tombstones extending forever.

"... Right to have—how would they say it? To have 'cancelled' us." She laughed a little, which became a series of jagged coughs. "And Calvin ... Calvin is wrong. About you. About me. About everyone."

She shifted her head slightly, looking at the whole mural. "We ... we were *meant* to burn."

I angled my head to look at her; at the dark, smoldering eyes, the large, slightly mis-aligned teeth, even as she exhaled in a long, rattling breath, and just shrunk—like a bag with all the air sucked out; like a marionette lowered to the floor in an unrecognizable heap. After which I pressed my cheek to her own and just stayed that way, although for how long I couldn't possibly say. All I know is that I was 'awakened' by gunshots, by the *crack-crack* of small arms, followed by screaming; screaming and the instantly recognizable growls of dinosaurs—big ones, by the sound of it—which itself gave way to silence ... at which I knew, with a mixture of relief and anger (because it was too late for Fiona anyway), that the Norsemen were no more.

By the time I'd walked all the way back to the White House and the North Lawn—carrying Fiona's body on my shoulders—Calvin's announcement was well underway, although it came to an abrupt halt when I appeared near the scaffold and laid her at its feet; after which there were gasps followed by a hushed silence—that is, save for the ubiquitous crackling of the fire.

When at last Calvin spoke, he did so as someone who had already resigned himself to the harsh reality of her death, asking only if she had suffered, to which I responded, "No," and then inviting me to join him on the platform, which I did, climbing the rungs and taking his offered hand until we stood together over the crowd and the roaring pyre and he had turned to address his audience again.

"And so it goes," he said, simply, giving the moment time to breathe, allowing everyone to catch their breath, until someone unexpectedly shouted, "How did she die?" —at which he turned to me, humbly, impotently, I thought, and indicated I should step forward; which I did, stepping to the very edge of the platform and looking down at the flames and the upturned faces, liking the way it felt, liking the way it made my blood race and seemed to snap everything into focus, liking the sense of power and purpose.

"Norsemen," I said, bluntly, after which, having been a student of Calvin since before puberty, meaning I'd idolized him and observed him carefully in the hopes that I might one day be like him, I let the moment breathe—until, finally, I added, "They laid a trap ... and we blundered into it. And then they issued an ultimatum: Leave now. Leave, or die."

"Fuck them!" barked someone almost immediately, and was quickly joined by others—all of whom felt that retaliation should be swift as it was lethal.

"We outnumber them five to one! I say we do it now, while it's dark, and we have the element of surprise!"

At which Calvin quickly tugged me back and we changed places, so that I was standing behind him as he said, "Now wait just a minute, gang, just hold that line of thought. Because, see, the thing is, we *are* in their territory. All right? They warned us and we— well, we rightfully ignored them, because, as you say," He pointed at one of the teenagers, "We outnumbered them. By about five to one, as you say. But that's because we—we had a *job* to do. We had to come here and ... and burn what remained of the Old World, the old ways. But the Burning is done, don't you understand? We've done what we set out to do, we've burned it *fucking all!*"

He looked left and right quickly, as though to fan the flames—taking them all in, seeking to build momentum. When no one spoke up he said, "And that's why I think it's time to ... to consider a new way. A new paradigm, as they say. A new, well, a new purpose. A way—"

"Our purpose is to burn!" shouted someone near the front, an expression which was met with cheers and sustained applause, and at least one horse whistle.

"Yes! Yes, it is!" Calvin shouted back, and hastened to add, "And so you have! So you have. And so very, very brightly, I might add. But there comes a time when ... when Time itself—begins to *mutate.* When your mind and your body begin to change, to *evolve.*"

"It's called getting old!" someone shouted, and was met by laughter.

"It's also called adapting; just bending ever so slightly so that instead of blowing you over the wind becomes an *ally,* a source of energy, and a renewable one at that. What I'm saying is ... the Burn is over. That the fields have been thoroughly cleansed and prepped. And that it's time to ... to build again. It's time to re-learn farming, irrigation, how to brew beer, for God's sake! Because the keg—the keg eventually runs out. And that's because what we're doing here isn't sustainable. It—it never was. *But.* But. You wanted a leader ... and somehow you found me. And so it was up to me in those first dark days to lift you up and to bolster your spirits, to channel your energy, to keep you busy and just get you through it." He sounded fatherly, patriarchal. "To help you let go of what was—and will never be again."

He turned toward me suddenly, I don't know why. "So ... no. There will be no retaliation. Not against the Norsemen, nor any other group. And there will be no more destruction." And then he held out his hand—I'm still not sure why—and I just looked at it; wondering if he knew, somehow—if he had intuited it. That Fiona and I had lain together; that I was beginning to doubt his wisdom and his leadership, just as she had. That's when I noticed his hand was shaking slightly, as I had seen the hands of the very old and infirm do, and when I looked to his face I could see it—the age, the wear and tear, the lines just beginning to form around his eyes and his mouth, the hint of darkness just above his cheeks. But then he shook his hand as though urging me to take it and I did—grasping it firmly, assuredly—and we pulled each other into an embrace, a right bear hug, slapping each other on the back, seeming to acknowledge what we had in common, which, I was beginning to suspect, was a penchant for leadership. And Fiona.

But then I lifted my gaze over his shoulder—following the billowing embers, as I recall—and saw that great and terrible borealis in the sky and the dark shapes within it; saw the lights which shifted and bled in and out of each other and the alien colors which were not colors at all as we knew them but rather facets of some strange and inconceivable prism, and knew, even before I looked, that I would see those same colors in the eyes of the children below—the lost children, the children of the Flashback—just as I had seen them in the eyes of the dinosaurs which now ruled the earth. And more, that if I were to look, I'd see them in my own. And that's when I slid the shard of glass out of my back pocket (the one I'd kept as a keepsake after making love to Fiona) and, clasping it in both hands—so that it cut me deep before anyone else—drove it into Calvin's lower back.

At which Time stopped. It didn't mutate; it didn't evolve and transform—it just stopped; for I, and I alone, had stopped it. And then I was jerking Calvin against me, violently, brutally, again and again, sinking the shard deep into his flesh, using it to impale his spine, until he began coughing up blood—which gurgled darkly in the twilight and for the briefest of moments made one giant bubble—before releasing him completely and letting him fall backward into the fire, where he impacted like a fresh log, causing embers to explode upward, and began screaming—hideously, obscenely. Briefly.

"Salud!" cried everyone below at once, raising their fists in solidarity, even as I looked at the sky yet again and considered what I saw there, and what I had seen of myself; as I considered

what I had seen in the M.I.M. Museum and in Fiona's dying eyes.

You wanted a fresh start, I said to them, the lights, the shapes *within* the lights. *You wanted to cleanse away the old. Let us help you.*

And then I looked at my friends, at my people, my *tribe,* seeing the Flashback in their eyes and knowing, at last, that this was its final expression; that we were meant to burn and to be burned, to end everything we'd ever touched; to end it all and to finally end ourselves. To just walk into the fire and close the book for good. To fertilize the fields for whatever was to come next.

To burn and to burn brightly.

To burn and to be burned, briefly.

CONTRIBUTORS

Brad Petit was born in Washington, D.C., in the same hospital as Duke Ellington. You might recognize his writing from Impossible Task, Press Pause, the Raleigh News & Observer, or elsewhere. He now lives in South Carolina with his wife and son. His neighbors include a rock band, a barred owl, a few quiet churches, and several raccoons.

Mary Jo Rabe grew up on a farm in eastern Iowa, got degrees from Michigan State University and the University of Wisconsin-Milwaukee. She worked in the library of the Archdiocese of Freiburg, Germany, for 41 years and retired to Titisee-Neustadt, Germany. She has published "Blue Sunset", inspired by *Spoon River Anthology* and *The Martian Chronicles,* electronically and has been published in *Pulphouse, Fiction River, Penumbric Speculative Fiction, Alien Dimensions, Fabula Argentea, Dark Horses Magazine,* and other magazines and anthologies.

Lamont A. Turner's work has appeared in numerous online and print venues including *Mystery Weekly, Mystery Tribune, Cosmic Horror Monthly, Dark Dossier,* and other magazines, podcasts and anthologies. My short story collection, "Souls In A Blender" was released by St. Rooster Books in October 2021.

Cedrick May (he/him) is a writer, filmmaker, and teacher who lives in the Dallas/Fort Worth area. After nearly two decades of writing academic books and essays, he has returned to his first and foremost love--writing speculative fiction. In particular, he writes horror, supernatural thrillers, and tales of the weird West. Cedrick has published stories in *Aphelion* and the anthology, *Road Kill: Texas Horror by Texas Writers, volume 7.*

Jennifer Walker is a writer and doctor. Her short stories can be read in issues of *Not One of Us, Arcturus Magazine,* and *Eclectica Magazine,* among others. She lives in the Virgin Islands with her girlfriend and their two exquisitely beautiful and understandably narcissistic dogs.

Chris Riley lives near Sacramento, California, vowing one day to move back to the Pacific Northwest. In the meantime, he teaches special education, writes cool stories, and hides from the blasting heat for six months of the year. He has had over 100 short stories published in various magazines and anthologies, and across various genres. He is the author of the literary suspense novels *The Sinking of the Angie Piper* (Coffeetown Press, 2017) and *The Broken Pines* (forthcoming), and his debut short story collection of weird fiction is pending publication with Mount Abraxas Press. For more information, go to www.chrisrileyauthor.com.

Joseph Hirsch has sold work to numerous outlets, including *Unsettling Reads, The Western Online,* and *Zahir: A Journal of Speculative Fiction.* His stories have also appeared in *3 AM Magazine.* His nonfiction works have been featured in *Film International, Terror House,* and *Bull: Men's Fiction.* He lives in Cincinnati, Ohio and is online @ www.joeyhirsch.com

Judith Pancoast is the scary version of Grammy-nominated children's musician Judy Pancoast. Judith has collaborated with Joe R Lansdale and Keith Lansdale to adapt Joe's novella, "Christmas with the Dead," as a stage musical. Her short story, "The Ding-Ding," narrated by her, was featured on The Dark Tome podcast . In addition, three of her short stories have been published in *Northern Frights, the Journal of the Horror Writers of Maine,* and her story "The Devil Under the Stairs" was published in *Scary Snippets Vol. 6.* She lives with her husband and two rescue cats and a rescue dog in Southern

Connecticut and is an active member of the Horror Writers Association.

William Curnow's fiction has appeared in a number of magazines and anthologies, including *Weird Horror Magazine, Supernatural Tales, Egaeus Press* and *Jurassic London.* He lives in London.

Wayne Kyle Spitzer is an American writer, illustrator, and filmmaker. He is the author of countless books, stories and other works, including a film (*Shadows in the Garden*), a screenplay (*Algernon Blackwood's The Willows*), and a memoir (*X-Ray Rider*). His work has appeared in *MetaStellar—Speculative fiction and beyond, subTerrain Magazine: Strong Words for a Polite Nation* and *Columbia: The Magazine of Northwest History,* among others. He holds a Master of Fine Arts degree from Eastern Washington University, a B.A. from Gonzaga University, and an A.A.S. from Spokane Falls Community College. His recent fiction includes *The Man/Woman War* cycle of stories as well as the *Dinosaur Apocalypse Saga.* He lives with his sweetheart Ngoc Trinh Ho in the Spokane Valley.

9 7 9 8 3 7 1 6 3 8 8 6 1